CRIMSON CROWN

CRIMSON CROWN

A DYSTOPIAN VAMPIRE FANTASY ROMANCE

AMY PATRICK

Oxford South Press

CONTENTS

ABOUT

CRIMSON CROWN

The Crimson Court is at a turning point.

Abigail Byler's life is about to change profoundly... or end for good. It remains to be seen what will become of the vampire queen, Imogen.

And Abbi's eternal love, Reece, faces the possibility of taking on a job he was never meant to have while living without the only girl he's ever loved.

In this fourth and final installment of the Crimson Accord series, the fates of both the vampire and human races are at stake, and it all depends on *who* will wear the Crimson Crown.

Enjoy the exciting conclusion to the Crimson series!

Sign up now for Amy Patrick's VIP List and get a **free** book, exclusive content, and other fun freebies, plus book and sale news!

<u>**Join the VIP list here:**</u> https://bit.ly/APsVIPs

Keep in touch with Amy Patrick on Facebook, Instagram, Tiktok, Goodreads, Bookbub, and Pinterest!

The Crimson Accord Series
Crimson Born
Crimson Storm
Crimson Bond
Crimson Crown

The Hidden Saga
Hidden Deep (free ebook)
Hidden Heart
Hidden Hope
The Sway (FREE when you join my list!)
Hidden Darkness (Dark Court, 1)
Hidden Danger (Dark Court, 2)
Hidden Desire (Dark Court, 3)
Hidden Game (Ancient Court, 1)
Hidden Magic (Ancient Court, 2)
Hidden Hero (Ancient Court, 3)
Hidden Heir

1

SISTERS

Hampshire, *England 1835*

Father would positively murder me if he could see me now.

No, actually, he'd have his servant Thomas do it. Heaven forbid the Earl of Pembury get his soft nobleman's hands dirty.

Will's hands are definitely *not* soft, thanks to his work on my father's estate and here in the stables where he cares for our horses and maintains the carriages.

And I *like* him dirty.

Pulling him away from the carriage he's polishing, I lead the tall, muscular young stable hand to a shadowed corner of the carriage room and press myself against him, heedless of the perspiration stains his damp chest and abdomen will leave on my light cotton summer gown.

It's not the first time I've come to seek him out at the stables. Will grew up here at Stony Hill Park with Sadie and me. The youngest of my father's servants, he came to work on the estate at the age of ten.

We played together as children. Now, at the age of seventeen, our games have changed.

"Imogen, what are you doing?"

In spite of his words, Will knows very well what I want him to do and doesn't bother resisting the pressure of my fingers on his nape.

Glancing around first to make sure we're alone, he dips his head and kisses me.

His lips are hot and demanding, and the boredom and frustration of my stifling day-to-day existence fades away. There is only the taste of him and the feel of his firm body against mine and the hungry sounds he's making.

My heart is pounding, and my knees are threatening to give way. I hold Will tighter, partially for support and partially because times like this with him are always so fleeting. It's hard to get away from the house for long, and he's always working, sunup to sundown.

Lack of opportunity is why we've never gone farther than kissing. That, and the aforementioned likelihood of murder. If not mine, then certainly Will's. I don't want to endanger him, but I also can't seem to stay away.

And Father isn't home at the moment. He's away in London on business.

Perhaps that's why I'm feeling braver than usual. As we kiss, I tug at the hem of Will's shirt, freeing it from the waist of his trousers, sliding my hands underneath and greedily caressing the steamed skin of his abdomen and back.

He lets out a tortured groan and breaks the kiss, panting quietly against my lips. "Imogen. Don't do that. You know we can't."

"Yes, we can." I pout. "I love you, and you love me. And who cares if I'm a virgin?"

He huffs a laugh. "I believe your father, the earl, cares

very much. Or he *will* when the grand lord you marry finds out on his wedding night he's been handed a soiled dove."

"It'll serve both of them right," I spit out. "My father and whichever decrepit old man he barters me to. It'll probably be some widower with children a decade older than me. And it's not *my* fault Father mismanaged his inheritance and ran the estate into the ground."

It's a poorly kept secret the earl is approaching a state of desperation.

While large and elegantly appointed, our country manor home is on a gradual slide toward disrepair. Our town home in London is woefully understaffed as Father let go some of the help to conserve funds, and the last time Sadie and I went to the modiste in the city for new dresses, the woman carried on a not-so-discreet conversation with her assistants about how late Father was in paying his account with her.

Like many titled Englishmen, my father inherited land and homes with his prestigious title but precious little money to maintain them all.

Noblemen don't work, of course. It's considered beneath the members of first society. And there are only so many socially acceptable ways to infuse an impoverished crumbling estate with cash.

Marrying your daughters to peers with deeper pockets is the current favorite.

"Still..." Will says, looking at me with obvious regret. "We should stop. I have work to do."

I grab the braces of his pants and pull him toward me again. "Work can wait. I can't. I want you. Kiss me again. Please."

His resolve crumbles, as I knew it would, and he takes me in his arms again, kissing me with renewed fervency. Holding me tightly against him, he turns us so I'm pinned between the wall and his body—exactly where I want to be.

I renew my efforts to get his shirt off, unbuttoning it as he begins to gather my long skirts, working them upward.

"Imogen?"

A confused sounding female voice breaks the quiet and causes us to spring apart in surprise.

Turning toward the doorway, I glare at the person who has, all our lives, been in possession of the world's worst timing.

My sister.

If I had my hand in the cookie tin, you could practically guarantee Sadie would wander into the cook's pantry and catch me. If I ever sneaked out of the house at night to look at the stars or hunt frogs with Will, Sadie would inevitably have a nightmare and come to my room for comfort then alert the entire household I'd been "kidnapped," prompting a search party.

"What do you want?" I demand.

"Father has returned from London. He's looking for you. He wants to speak to us both together."

My sister folds her hands primly in front of her and averts her innocent gaze as Will turns toward the opposite wall and hurriedly rebuttons his shirt, tucking it back into his trousers.

"He has the housekeeper in a tizzy, and all the footmen are out combing the estate grounds for you," Sadie informs me. "I thought it would be best for them not to find you... like this."

Setting my own clothing to rights, I stride toward her. "Like what? Having fun? Having a life? If it were up to Father, all we'd do is sit in the parlor all day writing letters and doing embroidery."

"That is what the daughters of noblemen do. We're lucky to live a refined life where we have time to pursue—"

"Husbands," I interrupt. "That's all we're allowed to

pursue. And we're hardly lucky. Father wants to marry you off to Lord Hertsford, who's positively ancient and has a goiter the size of his head. And Mother told me he has his eye on another dusty old duke for me. Well, no thank you. I don't want any of it."

When Will's fully dressed again, he comes to stand beside me, giving my sister a sheepish grin. "Hello Sadie."

"Hello William. The carriage looks wonderful. You've done such a good job on it."

"Don't talk to him like a servant," I snap.

"But he is a..." Sadie cuts herself off, pasting on a demure smile. "Do excuse us, William. Our father has requested our presence in his office, and we must go at once."

He gives her a half-bow. "Of course, my lady." Then he turns and goes back to the carriage, lifting the polishing cloth from its lantern hook and resuming his work without another glance in my direction.

Obedient. Dutiful. I want to throw up.

Just to make a point, I go to him and plant a goodbye kiss on his cheek before joining my sister for the walk to the house.

She says nothing about it. Or the fact she caught us groping in a dark corner. And she doesn't ask for gratitude over the fact she prevented *someone else* from catching us groping in a dark corner.

It irritates me that I *am* grateful. It's even more irritating to see yet another bit of evidence of just how honorable she is.

Ever the rule-follower, Sadie fell right into line and started playing the role of wellborn lady as soon as she turned seventeen and was presented to society for her first season.

She should have been snatched up off the marriage market immediately. With her English rose beauty and her perfect manners and her natural sweetness, she's exactly what every nobleman wants in a wife.

Unfortunately—for her—our family name carries with it the thing English noblemen want *least*—debt. Only those with the oldest and richest estates could afford to marry one of us.

That is the only reason Sadie has gone through two London seasons without a single marriage offer and, at the age of nineteen, is rapidly heading for spinsterhood.

I've only had to endure one season so far, and I was thrilled when it turned out to be just as "unsuccessful" (Father's word, not mine) as Sadie's had been.

Mother is a different story. She sees our wallflower status as her failure, and Father doesn't discourage that conclusion. Mother was so upset after the final ball of the season that she left for a tour of the continent with her sisters.

As we do each summer, Sadie and I retreated to our estate in the country. I couldn't wait to get back to its relative peace and freedom. And to Will.

Instead of coming with us, Father stayed behind in London to conduct "business" of some sort. I'd hoped it would last several weeks, at least, but apparently a few additional days was all he'd needed to spend there.

"When did he arrive?" I ask Sadie.

"An hour ago. He took a hired coach. Apparently he was quite in a hurry to get here for some reason."

"Do you have any idea why he wants to see us?"

In noble families like ours, parents—particularly fathers—don't spend much time with their children—particularly daughters. It's the servants who do most of the childrearing, and even though Sadie and I are no longer young girls, we rarely see our father. He certainly doesn't summon us to his office often.

"I don't know, but I overheard the housekeeper talking to

one of the kitchen maids," Sadie answers. "She said something about a ball."

"A ball. Here? Do you think he means to hold a house party?"

While I have little interest in the endless succession of stuffy London balls, summer house parties are another thing entirely. Guests come and inhabit the manor's ample guest rooms for weeks at a time, and there are lawn games and trail walks and hunting parties during the day and festive dinners and dancing at night.

Most house parties begin with a welcoming ball. It seems odd Father would plan such an event in Mother's absence though.

"We'll find out his plans soon enough, I suppose," Sadie says.

We reach the house, a romantic, gothic mansion fronted with towering columns and tall Palladian windows that want cleaning, as do the ten chimney stacks and the white exterior which once gleamed like snow but has now dulled to an eggshell tone.

Inside we traverse the marble entrance hall floor and ascend the grand staircase to the second level, walking down a long, carpeted hallway to the heavy wooden door of Father's office.

Sadie raps lightly on it with her knuckles.

Father's gruff voice comes from within. "Enter."

My sister and I step into the dark, masculine room with its heavy brocade draperies and forest green silk wall panels. Father sits behind a large cherrywood desk where he works by the light of a single lamp. A ledger book lies open in front of him, and a deep furrow bisects his brow.

He stands as we come to a stop in front of his desk. The crease in his forehead doesn't relax as he looks us each over with an assessing eye.

I once thought of my father as a tall man, but as I've matured, I've realized it's only his extreme leanness that makes him appear so. He's actually of average height.

With his slight build, one might take him for a younger man at a distance, but up close like this it's possible to see the evidence of years of worry and disappointment etched on his face.

And then his face brightens with a rare smile. "Daughters. I have excellent news of great importance, and it concerns you both."

Inviting us to sit in the uncomfortable hardbacked chairs in front of his desk, he explains.

"There is to be a ball here in three days. Our neighbors from the other Hampshire estates will be in attendance, as will a special guest."

A special guest? That's intriguing. And based on Father's expression this guest is quite special indeed.

"Who is it, Father? A member of the royal family?" I ask.

He smiles again. "Even better. He is a foreign prince, from Moldavia, and he's in need of a wife. I made his acquaintance at my club in London, and he's very eager to meet you both."

Sadie sits back in her chair, staying silent, as well-bred young ladies are expected to do. I scoot forward to the edge of my chair.

"A prince! What is his name? How old is he? Where is Moldavia?"

In a rare moment of indulgence, Father answers each question. Even seems happy to do so.

"Moldavia is a principality in the Ottoman Empire, a small country but very wealthy. His name is Alexandru. I'm not certain of his exact age but he has the look of a twenty-five-year-old."

Sadie's eyes flare with surprise, though I'm the only one who says aloud what we're both thinking.

"Only twenty-five? He's young then." My heart leaps with hope. "And you say he's wealthy?"

Still grinning, Father slides a hand into his pocket and pulls it out again, opening it to reveal a handful of sparkling gemstones. I'm no expert, but they look like diamonds and rubies and emeralds, some of them quite large.

"Prince Alexandru gave them to me for safekeeping," he says. "He'll be traveling from London by carriage the night of the ball and didn't want to risk running into highwaymen who may have gotten word of his fortune."

It seems the furrow has jumped from Father's forehead to Sadie's. She finally speaks. "That is an... interesting request."

Father beams. "I think it shows great trust and confidence in my honorable nature. An auspicious beginning to an agreeable partnership. He says the rubies are particularly valuable. Blood rubies, he called them. His country is apparently quite rich with them. In fact, he requested I present each of you with one as a token of his esteem."

Shaking his hand side to side so the gemstones roll and flash in the lamplight, he says, "Go ahead. Choose one."

While I reach out and select the largest of the sparkling red stones, Sadie folds her fingers together on her lap.

"I'm not sure how he can hold us in high esteem when he hasn't yet met us," she says. "And it's improper to accept a gift from a gentleman we don't even know."

Father's usual sour demeanor snaps back into place.

"*I'll* be the judge of what's proper and improper. And three days from now you *will* know the gentleman. And you'll converse with him and dine with him and dance with him and do *whatever is necessary* to make him feel welcome. I won't have you insult him by refusing his generosity."

Shoving his hand in front of Sadie's face, he repeats. "Choose a stone, daughter. Perhaps it will become the centerpiece of your engagement ring. You *are* the one he's going to marry."

Wait, what?

Sadie's face shows no sign of surprise. Obviously she understood Father's meaning all along while it took me longer to catch on.

"You've arranged for *Sadie* to marry him?" I ask.

"Of course. She's the eldest—that's the way it's done. You *know* that. Besides, she's the most marriageable by far."

The sting of his disapproval and obvious preference for Sadie has long since ceased to faze me. I ignore it, focusing on the more pressing matter.

"But... you said he was eager to meet us both. And he instructed you to gift each of us with a gemstone."

Father laughs. "And he wants your mother to have one as well. He gave me a diamond cravat pin. As I've said, Prince Alexandru is very generous, and he wants to make a good impression on his new fiancée's family. Now go, both of you, and begin preparations. In your mother's absence, you are the lady of the house, Sadie. And you, Imogen, you will assist her in any way she needs to make this ball the finest Hampshire county has seen in years. We have much to celebrate. God has answered our prayers."

WHEN OUR "SPECIAL GUEST" arrives three nights later, I decide the Almighty has nothing to do with it.

Sadie and I huddle together behind the drawn drapes of an upstairs room, peering through the narrow opening between them at the man emerging from the opulent black lacquered carriage.

If there's anything angelic about Prince Alexandru, it's of

the *fallen* angel variety. He's the most wickedly handsome man I've ever seen.

Tall, dark-haired, and impeccably dressed in black and white formalwear, he exits the carriage with the lithe grace of a stalking cat. The predatory impression is reinforced by the way he turns side to side, scanning the drive and house as if prepared to launch into hand-to-hand battle at any moment.

"He looks... different than I expected," Sadie says, wearing a tiny frown.

"He looks dangerous," I say. And I'm finding *that* dangerously attractive.

Three women follow the prince out of the carriage and shake out their skirts. They're all exceptionally beautiful and dripping in jewels. Instead of pinning it up in the current fashion, they wear their hair long and loose.

Most remarkable of all, are their gowns. They're obviously finely made but shocking in color.

"They're wearing red," Sadie exclaims. "I wonder who they are? Father didn't say the prince would be accompanied."

"I'll bet they're his sisters. They must all be married."

Societal norms restrict young unmarried women such as ourselves to white gowns or the palest pastels. Even the older matrons generally stick to subdued shades.

These women stand out. They remind me of the bright cardinals that give life to the stark white landscape during the dreariest of winter doldrums.

"I wonder where their husbands are?" Sadie asks.

"Perhaps back in Moldavia? If they're married at all."

"Even if they *are* married, the color is scandalous, especially for a country house party. Especially for a first-time meeting," Sadie says.

Irritated by her ever-present sense of propriety, I say, "I

think they look exquisite. Perhaps in their country all the young ladies wear red to match those beautiful blood rubies Father showed us. I wish *I* were going to live in Moldavia."

While pastels are the perfect complement to Sadie's blonde hair and cream-and-sugar complexion, my own pale skin and dark hair would look better against darker, more dramatic tones.

Sadie sniffs. "Well, if I become the princess of Moldavia, I *won't* be wearing shocking red, I can tell you that for certain."

Prince Alexandru speaks to his female companions, and they all move toward the manor's front entry steps. Just as he reaches the bottom step, he stops and looks up at the window, as if he knows he's being watched.

Sadie and I jump back so quickly we trip over each other's feet and end up in a heap on the rug. Then we start giggling uncontrollably.

"Do you think he saw us?" she asks with a mixture of horror and mirth.

I flop onto my back and stare up at the ceiling, savoring the memory of his unusual light eyes and shockingly sensual lips. "I don't think so, but *I* certainly saw *him*. Isn't he the most beautiful man you've ever laid eyes on?"

"'Tis only skin deep," my virtuous sister reminds me. "I shall reserve judgment on his beauty until I've gotten to know him better."

Sadie's chambermaid Lily comes in and makes a shocked noise at the sight of the two of us sprawled on the floor.

"Misses Sadie and Imogen, it's time to get you dressed. The guests are beginning to arrive. Your father won't like it if you're late."

Sadie gets to her feet, wearing a chastened grin. "I'm ready except for putting on my gown. Help Imogen. Her hair has fallen from its pins."

My hand goes to my head, and I realize she's right. Her

hair has somehow stayed perfectly in place, in spite of our roll on the rug. Of course.

"I have your dress all pressed and laid out for you, my lady," Lily says. "And I'll put the curling iron into the fire, so it'll be all hot and ready to repair your hair."

"Thank you, Lily." I get up and head for the door, turning back to speak to Sadie. "See you downstairs?"

"I'll come to your room when I'm dressed, and we'll go down together."

Suddenly, in spite of my earlier annoyance with her, I'm glad my sister will be at my side tonight. Now that I've seen them, the thought of meeting the dashing prince and his glamorous companions is rather intimidating.

Not that he'll even notice me. Next to my lovely sister and those vibrant women accompanying him, I'll be positively invisible. As usual.

Hurrying down the corridor toward my room, I pass the family parlor and then my parents' respective chambers.

Then I stop. I turn around and go back to the doorway of Mother's room, hesitating with my hand on the knob.

She's traveling abroad, of course, but she's never minded before when I entered her room. I open the door and go in, walking directly to the large wardrobe against one wall.

Did she leave it? I hope she left it.

Throwing open the heavy double doors, I do a quick scan of the clothing items left inside. *Yes.* There it is.

My mother has many beautiful gowns, but this one has always been my favorite. And she's never worn it. Has never dared.

Quickly, before I can think better of it, I grab the gorgeous dress she's labeled a "foolish flight of fancy" and an ill-advised "waste of coin" and best of all "a harlot's calling card."

Making sure not to step on the voluminous fabric in my

arms, I rush down the corridor to my room. I feel like someone's stepped on a hive of bees in my stomach, sending a buzz of excitement through every part of me.

Tonight... I will be *seen*.

Lily wisely keeps her mouth shut about my abrupt change of wardrobe, but I read the shock and censure in her eyes. Nevertheless, she helps me on with my corset and the daring flame-red dress.

Then she follows my instructions and styles my hair in a flowing cascade of curls, reminiscent of the women the prince arrived with. Unpinned like this, the dark locks fall halfway down my back.

As a final touch, I add a necklace from my jewelry case. It's a gold chain with a pendant at the end in the form of a hollow heart-shaped basket. I wear it frequently.

At times I've opened the little basket and put things inside. A fresh rosebud. A snip of cloth dabbed with perfume. A folded love note from Will.

Tonight, I have the perfect accessory in mind. Inserting the blood ruby into the golden basket, I snap it closed and let the pendant fall onto my chest where it nestles at the top of my pushed-up cleavage.

Then I inspect the complete ensemble in the full-length standing mirror. "How do I look, Lily?"

"Very... eye-catching, my lady."

I smile because that's exactly what I was hoping for.

I hear Sadie's gasp before I spot her behind me in the mirror. She's stopped stock-still in the doorway.

"*Whatever* are you wearing?"

I smirk at her shocked expression. "A ballgown. It's Mother's. Remember when she had it made and then was too timid to wear it anywhere? I'm *not* too timid. Shall we go down?"

"Your hair..." Sadie says. Though she fails to finish the

sentence, I know how it finishes. *Is inappropriate. Is wild and wanton. Isn't what I would do in a million years.*

"My hair matches the style of the prince's sisters. I'm sure he will approve."

She recoils and does a quick double-blink. "Do you *want* him to approve of you?"

"Of course," I say in a flippant tone. "Father did say we should do everything in our power to make Prince Alexandru feel welcome."

She rolls her eyes. "Including wearing a ridiculous costume? He may be foreign royalty, but he's just a man. And you're *not* foreign—or old enough—or *married* enough—to wear that color. You're a highborn English girl, Imogen. Not a Moldavian queen."

I laugh, taking my skirts in my hands and twirling in an exuberant spin.

"I think I'd make a *wonderful* queen."

2

WHERE WILL I GO

Abbi

Imogen's eyelids fluttered again.

She hadn't moved, hadn't spoken. None of us knew whether she was even aware of her surroundings yet.

One thing *was* certain. She was human.

Larkin's cure had worked. Though Imogen seemed to be drifting in and out of consciousness, we'd all seen her eyes. They were blue, not lilac-colored.

I shared a sideways glance with my friend, who wore an expression of concern instead of elation over her scientific success. Reaching over to grasp her hand, I squeezed it.

Larkin squeezed back and gave me a tremulous smile. "This is good news... right?"

I nodded. Though I wasn't sure what would happen next, it *wouldn't* be a mass execution of all my friends. If Imogen was no longer a vampire, she couldn't be queen of the vampires.

"This is good news," I assured her. "Vampirism can be cured."

"Good news for those who *want* to be cured," Kannon corrected in a sullen tone.

"Right."

The Bloodbound soldier had already made it clear he had no interest in becoming human again. As it would very likely mean a return to his human condition of waist-down paralysis, I understood.

Did *I* want to be cured? I still wasn't sure. I thought so.

Becoming a vampire hadn't been my choice, and my life since turning hadn't exactly been easy. But Reece insisted becoming a vampire—becoming *queen* of the vampires in this country—was my destiny.

Reece.

He was the real issue. He didn't *want* to go back to his human life, insisted there was nothing for him to go back to. And he wanted to make sure the vampire species had a leader and protection against the threat from the growing faction of humans who hated us just for being who we were.

If I reclaimed my humanity, it might mean losing him. That possibility was every bit as repellent to me as the idea of "ruling" over anyone and anything.

Where *was* he, by the way? I assumed he hadn't followed me here to the clinic because he'd been annoyed about my eagerness to check on Shane's condition. But Reece *needed* to know about this development with Imogen. It affected him as directly as it affected me.

"Do you know where Reece is?" I asked Kannon. "He should know about this."

Kannon smirked. "He took some of the guys and went out on a patrol, said he wanted to give you 'space' while you visited your human boyfriend and figured out what you wanted to do about him."

"Shane *isn't* my boyfriend. He isn't human either. Not anymore."

My friend, who'd helped me safely travel cross-country from California to the Bastion, had been rewarded for his kindness by being served up at a human feast thrown by Imogen. Reece, Larkin, and I had arrived in the nick of time to prevent his death.

Unfortunately the only way to save him had been to turn him. Since I'd refused, Reece had been the one to bite him, saying he didn't want me mourning Shane's death for eternity. It wasn't until tonight we'd learned it had worked.

"Do you think he'll want the cure? Obviously it works." Kannon threw a significant glance in Imogen's direction.

She was definitely waking up. She'd made a couple of moaning sounds, and her fingers and feet twitched. "Will," she mumbled in a barely audible voice. "Where's Will?"

"I doubt it," I said. "The love of Shane's life is here—she's a vampire—her name's Marjorie. I think they're both pretty excited about the idea of spending eternity together."

"Sweet," Kannon said.

Dr. Coppa moved close to the bed. "Would you all mind stepping out of the room please? I need to examine Imogen, and it would probably be better if the news about her... *changed* condition came from me rather than any of you."

The three of us moved into the hallway and kept our voices low.

"How do you think she'll take it?" Larkin asked.

Only someone who didn't know Imogen would ask that question.

Kannon and I spoke at once. "Not well."

He turned to me. "You should address the people as soon as possible. They need to know about the transfer of power."

Larkin corrected him. "Abbi hasn't made up her mind yet. She's not sure she wants the position of queen."

Kannon's head jerked back, and his face screwed up in confusion as he glanced between my friend and me. "What?

It's not a matter of want or don't want. You *are* queen, Abbi. You have to lead us in the war against President Parker and his followers. You have to start giving the Bloodbound your blood. We'll fall apart without it. Imogen's blood will start wearing off in a matter of days. The troops won't stay loyal without it."

A wave of heat passed through me, and I brought shaky hands up to hold my own face. "This is all happening too fast. A few minutes ago, I was seriously considering turning human again. Now suddenly I'm supposed to be queen? And give people my blood to drink to, what—hypnotize them? Drug them?"

Larkin spoke up. "Look, I know I'm new here and don't understand the way it all works, but maybe it isn't necessary. Maybe the vampire race won't even *need* a queen anymore, you know? Now we know the cure is effective. If I had a lab to work in and some help, I could produce enough for everyone."

Kannon glared at her. "Not everyone here wants a cure. Some of us can't go back to being human, and if the overall number of us is reduced, what happens to the rest of us, huh? We'll never achieve equality with humans if we're a tiny minority. They'll lose their motivation to work with us if they're no longer afraid."

The debate was ended by Dr. Coppa opening the door. "You can come in now," he said. "*if* you want to."

The look on his face told me he'd rather be almost anywhere else. The reason for that was obvious once we filed back into the room.

Imogen was thrashing about on the bed, ripping the white sheets and screaming. When she spotted me, she leapt to the floor and came toward me, not stopping until our faces were inches apart.

"This is *your* doing. How *dare* you think you could steal

my throne. I regret ever gifting you with immortality. I should have let you bleed out on that deserted road—or better yet, drained you myself. Well, you're not going to get away with it."

She shifted her gaze to Kannon. "Kill her."

He stayed in place, rolling his lips inward in an uncomfortable expression before looking away toward the clinic wall.

Imogen's nostrils flared in fury. "Have you lost your hearing or just your manhood? I don't care if you are 'friends,' your *queen* has given you an order. Kill her. Now."

Now he looked at her. "I can't do that. You're not my queen anymore."

For a moment she stood dumbstruck. Then she looked at Dr. Coppa, who nodded in confirmation.

"I'm afraid it won't be safe for you to stay at the Bastion. Your blood... well, it would be too tempting for too many."

Kannon added, "You can't lead the vampire race if you're not a vampire. The people won't follow you. Neither will the Bloodbound."

Imogen slapped him with a loud crack. Kannon barely flinched.

Apparently at a loss, Imogen went still and silent for a moment, during which a progression of thoughts was clear on her face. She went from shock, to concern, to understanding, and back to fury.

When she spoke again, she was sputtering. "What will I do now? Where will I go? I have no money, no home."

She glared at me as if it was my fault.

"Normally, I'd suggest someone in your position stay with family for a while," I said. "Unfortunately you murdered yours."

3

———

PUT IT ON

Abbi

"It wasn't me," Imogen said.

Standing in her bare feet on the clinic floor, glancing from one to the other of us with pleading eyes, she seemed smaller than she'd ever been.

She still looked pretty much the same—young and beautiful, with long, dark hair and luminous skin—a dead ringer for Audrey Hepburn. But she was diminished in every other way—in pride, in power, in self-assurance.

"I didn't have Sadie killed," she insisted. "We had our differences over the years, but I decided to just let her live out her days in hiding."

I wasn't sure if she was telling the truth or just trying to cover her butt now that her power was gone and she was vulnerable. My money was on the latter.

"You sent Reece to assassinate her," I said.

"I did, but I reconsidered after you two left. I was going to tell him when he checked in with me, but it was already too late. In the end, I decided family mattered most."

Lunging toward Kannon, she grabbed the dagger from

his belt and whirled back to face me, advancing toward me with the wickedly sharp blade and sneering.

"I won't make that mistake again... *daughter.*"

Thankfully, Imogen's vampire speed was no longer present. Kannon stepped in front of me, easily blocking her path in time. I was worried she'd stab him instead, but that didn't happen.

With a scream, she dropped the knife.

At first, I thought she was simply frustrated and giving up because she realized the futility of her actions. Kannon was so much larger and stronger. But then she crumpled to the floor.

She writhed there, letting out an ungodly howl. *What* was going on? Was she having a tantrum?

"What's the matter with her?" I asked, trying to peer around Kannon's large form. "What's happening?"

He held his arms out to the side to keep me safely behind him. "Stay back. This could be another one of her tricks."

A minute later, all noise and motion ceased as Imogen went silent and still. Everyone in the room stared, watching and waiting for another sneak attack.

Then Dr. Coppa launched into action, moving toward her and dropping to his knees beside her. He placed two fingers to her carotid artery.

He looked up at us, his forehead creased. "She's dead."

"What?" Larkin rushed to his side and crouched beside Imogen's motionless body, feeling for a pulse in her limp wrist. "Are you sure?"

The doctor nodded. Apparently not finding a pulse, Larkin let Imogen's hand fall to the floor.

I'd seen vampires die of beheading. I'd seen the piles of ash left over from a few who'd chosen to daylight themselves. But I'd never seen one die of old age.

We watched as Imogen's body decomposed, sinking into

itself and shrinking with every passing minute until all that was left was a horrific skeletal version of the woman.

After all the terror she'd inspired and all the havoc she'd wreaked in her life, it was over. She was gone.

"Oh my God," I gasped. "Why did that happen?"

Larkin shook her head, her brows pulled tightly together as she stared down at the mummified corpse. "I'm not sure. It must have been an effect of the cure."

Dr. Coppa nodded in agreement. "I think when her humanity returned, her real age caught up with her."

My stomach clenched, and my eyelids dropped closed. "Then it's not going to work for any of the older vampires."

After another second it hit me. "What about those who turned after being gravely injured... like me? Do you think our human injuries would return along with our humanity?"

Larkin gave me a sorrowful glance. "I don't know. Maybe. It's too risky to find out though. Who would volunteer for a trial?"

"I would," I blurted.

Kannon practically shouted, "No." Then he followed it up by explaining, "She's too important to our people."

Larkin nodded rapidly. "Of course. I wasn't thinking of her."

"All of our people are important," I argued. "Why shouldn't I be the one to test it?"

Kannon pulled me to the side, speaking in a low voice. "See, *this* is why you'll be a great leader. You're willing to sacrifice yourself for others. It's not the time and place though. If Larkin is going to do any further research, she'll need support. *You* can give that to her better than anyone but only if you accept the mantle of queen."

I was quiet for a moment, considering it. On my own I had no money, no power, no ability to help.

Dammit.

"You're right." I sighed. "She'll need help and resources, and I can only give that to her if I'm in a position of leadership."

My hope was I wouldn't have to stay in the position for long. As soon as we got a cure that would work for everyone, a vampire queen *wouldn't* be necessary. I planned to give Larkin all the help she needed to make that happen.

Unaware of my inner escape-hatch thoughts, Kannon visibly relaxed, his rigid posture loosening along with his tense facial muscles.

"Great. I'll arrange an assembly of the population in the Grand Dome. Imogen's official records and the crown are in her chambers—I mean *your* new chambers."

Everything was changing so fast I felt like my head spun. "What am I supposed to do with them?"

"You'll need to take the records to Eudora to be preserved, now that Imogen's reign has ended. You'll also need to consult with her about the right amount of queensblood to mix into the Bloodbound's rations. I never watched Imogen do it, but Eudora's been around a *long* time. She'll know. As for the crown... you should put it on."

He smiled. I couldn't return the gesture.

"I'm not too sure about that part. When do you think Reece will get back?"

"Hard to say. They went radio silent a little while ago—tracking down a rogue and didn't want the radios to spook him. I'll tell him to get back here to base the minute I hear from him."

4

THE WAY IT'S ALWAYS
BEEN DONE

Abbi

It was an otherworldly feeling, entering Imogen's chambers—former chambers.

Every other time I'd been here, the calcite walls of this cavern had seemed to pulse with malice.

Now... it was just a set of rooms, decorated with items she'd collected from her travels around the world—things I'd never have chosen for myself. If I were planning to stay, which I wasn't, I supposed I'd start a collection of my own and have all these priceless relics removed.

Maybe I'd go ahead and do it anyway—the removal part. They probably should go into the archives with Imogen's records.

The Bastion *did* have a museum, filled with art pieces depicting vampires throughout history as well as carefully preserved and framed news headlines and articles from the 1960s when Sadie and President Kennedy had signed the Crimson Accord and vampires had finally emerged from the shadows and into public life.

The personal art collection of a former queen would be an appropriate addition.

So would the Crimson Crown—once it was no longer necessary.

I studied the bejeweled headpiece on its stand in an alcove. Comprised of onyx and ruby red jewels, it sparkled darkly in the candlelight.

It looked... heavy.

Shaking off a shiver, I moved to a tall antique cabinet with glass doors—my mother would have called a piece of furniture like this a "secretary." Behind the panes of glass were rows of books, including the leatherbound journals that held Imogen's records and private notes from her time as queen.

Though I was alone in the room, I glanced back over my shoulder before opening the bookcase, as if I was a naughty child sneaking Mamm's homemade candies from the box in the cupboard.

Carefully, I removed the record books containing Imogen's flowing cursive script. The sheer number of them spoke to the length of her reign.

Then with Kannon and another guard, I headed for the Bastion's archives where Eudora served as the community's historian—when she wasn't teaching newly turned vampires.

Kannon knocked. After a few moments, the heavy door opened. The ancient historian's eyes went wide at the site of us and our cargo.

From the expression on her face, she understood instantly what our visit meant. She bent at the waist and dipped her head low.

"My queen. Please come in."

It was bizarre to have the distinguished elderly woman who'd been my instructor when I'd first arrived now bow to me. Bizarre and very uncomfortable.

I entered the room but corrected her. "I'm still just Abigail."

Eudora's eyes squinted, and her head cocked to the side as she threw a glance at the collection of journals. "You are not queen then? Imogen lives?"

"No, you're right about that—she *is* dead," I confirmed. "I'm about to hold a gathering and tell everyone... something. I'm not quite sure *what* to say to them."

My stomach somersaulted every time I thought about standing in front of the whole population of the Bastion. What *would* I say, assuming I could get any words out at all?

Eudora stayed stoic, not seeming surprised or alarmed to hear of Imogen's demise.

"Well then, you *are* my queen," she informed me. "I know she was angry with you when you left, but she made it clear you had queensblood. You're back now. All hives must have a queen. If Imogen's dead, then it's you. You're her heir. There is no one else."

A new surge of terror washed down my spine.

"I know. It just... feels a little weird right now. And I'm not sure I'm really the right person for the job," I told her. "I'm still making up my mind about whether I'll even *stay* on the throne."

"Making up your mind?" She let out a loud snort of laughter. "Destiny has made up *its* mind on your behalf. If you want to abdicate the throne, you'd better get busy with your drones and create a little princess."

She gave Kannon a lecherous look that was comical considering she appeared to be about a hundred and was in actuality much, much older. "This one looks like *he* could get the job done."

A shocked look crossed his face. Apparently it hadn't yet occurred to him what it would mean if the tradition of the queen mating with all her Bloodbound soldiers continued with me in place of Imogen.

He was thinking of it now.

The two of us exchanged wide-eyed glances and then headshakes of tacit agreement. *That would be a hard no.* For one thing, neither of us was interested in each other that way. For another, if we *were,* Reece would murder his friend.

"Mustn't play favorites though," Eudora went on, oblivious to the unspoken conversation going on between Kannon and me. "You'll need to spend time with *all* your Bloodbound to improve your chances of conceiving. The sooner the better—you'll start tonight if you're smart."

I concluded it was a very good thing Reece *was* out on patrol right now and not here to overhear the elderly vampire's advice.

"Isn't there another way?" I asked her. "Surely with all your years as historian... well, there must be another... option."

She nodded, motioning for me to hand over the journals, which I did.

"That's the way it's always been, and the way it always must be," Eudora said. "You *could* do what Imogen did. Search for a girl with the right pheromone combination, and when you find her, turn her. Train her and let her take on the responsibility. Could take some time though. Imogen looked for decades before finding you."

Ugh. Besides the time factor, it didn't feel right to foist this burden off on some other poor girl.

Not for the first time I found myself asking, *What would Sadie do?* I wished I had *her* journals to consult instead of Imogen's. If I had to be a leader, I wanted to be one like my old mentor, not like the woman who'd turned me.

"What if the vampires *had* no queen?" I asked, desperate for a way out of this. "What if there was like, a governing committee or something? Or a spokesperson, like Sadie Aldritch was with the VHC?"

"That particular organization was about peace, was it not?" Eudora asked. "And look how that turned out. Poor Sadie. What she never understood was being an effective leader is about *power*. And you, my dear, *are* powerful—never doubt it. I've seen a lot of queens come and go, and your power is among the greatest. Your only challenge will be deciding how to wield it and when.

She carried the stack of journals to a tall bookcase and began climbing the ladder leaned against it.

"As far as whether vampires can get along without a queen, you only need to look to bee colonies for the answer."

Eudora slid each of the books, one after the other, into an empty spot on one of the higher shelves.

"Without a queen bee, the worker bees become agitated and aggressive," she said. "The whole colony becomes vulnerable and cannot survive for long. You *could* simply do away with the hive, with the Bastion, altogether, but the outside world isn't exactly a hospitable place right now."

Backing down the ladder, she stepped to the floor and turned to face me.

"In my opinion, this hive is more necessary now than it's ever been at any time in history." She shrugged. "But of course the decision is up to you. Just keep this in mind... any mistakes you might make in ruling the people will pale in comparison to the damage you'll do by deciding *not* to rule."

Kannon and I excused ourselves and walked back toward my new quarters so I could prepare for the public address. When we reached them, it was obvious word had started to get around. The guards on duty bowed when they saw me.

At my invitation, Kannon followed me over the threshold into the receiving room. He hung back near the door. "It already feels different in here. I can't believe she's gone."

I turned to him. "Are you sorry she is?"

"Well, I can't say I'll miss her exactly. I'm just wondering what's next, you know?"

"You and me both. I feel so out of place here. And the thought of putting on that crown and going out there in front of the entire population of the Bastion makes me want to run up all those stairs till I reach the surface and keep going."

He chuckled. "You'll be fine. Just do your best impersonation of Imogen."

Ugh. That idea sent a wave of shudders through me. The last thing I wanted was to resemble Imogen. But I *could* do my best to act like Sadie did on the many occasions I'd seen her address a crowd.

"I'll just be honest with them," I told Kannon. "I'll just tell them what happened to Imogen and ask them for their patience and trust while we figure all this out together."

His face contracted in that I'm-not-so-sure-that's-a-good-idea squint. "Or... you could keep it short and sweet. Just tell them you're the new queen, let them see the Bloodbound following you, and they will too. Imogen certainly never explained herself."

He had a point. "Well, it probably doesn't matter too much *what* I say. The whole population will probably have heard what's happened before I can even tell them."

"They won't hear it from the Bloodbound," Kannon assured me. "You have their loyalty—for now at least. Reece and I will ensure it lasts until you can start giving the soldiers your queensblood in their rations. I noticed you didn't ask Eudora about the formula."

I walked around the room, studying the ornate antiques, priceless artwork, and luxurious rugs, wrinkling my nose at the red satin bedsheets.

"Maybe I spent too much time with Sadie, but it just feels

weird to coerce their obedience with my blood. How is that any different from drugging them?"

Kannon shrugged. "You just have to. You heard Eudora—it's the way it's always been done. Sometimes we're called to do things we'd rather not do. My grandma used to say, 'You don't know how strong you are until being strong is the only choice you have.'"

"Is she available?" I asked. "Sounds like she'd make an *excellent* queen."

5

TOTAL HONESTY

Reece

My team and I returned to the Bastion, tired, dirty, and more than a little frustrated about our failure to capture the rogue.

He'd been surprisingly fast and agile and had evaded us at every turn—kind of like I'd done when I was the rogue being hunted by a Bloodbound team.

Finally, we'd had to call it and head home before the sun came up.

We'd try again tomorrow night. The last thing we needed right now was a sloppy newbie vampire terrorizing the area surrounding the Bastion and drawing widespread attention.

Our stronghold was still a secret from our human enemies, and we couldn't risk the authorities congregating in this area and searching it.

If we were to lose this refuge, I wasn't sure what would happen to the refugees who'd come here and to all the vampire families who'd made the place their home.

It was the only place Abbi and her friends Kelly and Heather were safe now that they were wanted "criminals."

Speaking of, I could hardly wait to check in with Abbi. I missed her, and I didn't necessarily like the way we'd left things. Plus, I wanted to see if there'd been any change in Imogen's condition. And find out what the change in *Shane's* condition would mean for us.

Abbi had assured me she didn't want him—that I was the only one she wanted to be with.

But the way she'd jumped up and run to the clinic when someone had alerted her he was awake made me wonder.

When my team reached the entry chamber, I was surprised to hear the stalag-pipe organ chiming loudly through the caverns, its echoing tune signaling a summons to a gathering of the full community.

The other warriors and I fell into step with the crowds of chattering, whispering vampires streaming toward the Grand Dome. What did the impromptu gathering mean? And *who* had called it?

I looked around for Abbi. Was she still in the medical clinic with Shane?

Suddenly I hoped she had left the Bastion with him—or without him. If the cure had failed and Imogen had awakened still a vampire, this was the last place Abbi needed to be.

Yes, I wanted to be with her, but more than that, I wanted her to live. I wanted her to be safe. If that meant never seeing her again, then so be it.

My misery at being parted from her wasn't going to last long anyway. Imogen would *know* I'd broken my vows. She'd have me beheaded this very hour.

Which was just as well. I couldn't serve her any longer, and I'd *never* be able to "service" her as she expected all her Bloodbound to do eventually. I would literally rather die than be with anyone other than Abbi in that way.

The buzz of excitement in the Dome was more than a

sound. It was a palpable thing, spreading through the crowd like an electric current.

There had been rumors since the night of the "feast," and they'd multiplied each day that passed without a public appearance from Imogen.

Some said the shocking display of violence toward humans and Imogen's clear disregard for the consequences that night meant she was ready to launch her war on the humans.

Others, who'd spotted Abbi at the feast, speculated a coup was in the works. Kannon and I had done our best to maintain calm and control the past few days, but it wasn't easy—there was change brewing, and the vampire population of the Bastion could sense it.

When everyone was assembled, the door in the rear of the cavern opened. An elegant woman emerged wearing the Crimson crown and walking slowly toward the raised platform where the Crimson throne stood waiting.

My heart lurched into motion, banging against my sternum as if trying to escape my body.

She ascended the stairs to the throne and greeted her subjects with a breathtaking smile. Or maybe it was just me who couldn't breathe.

Abbi.

She was magnificent, resplendent in a floor-length red gown, the same one she'd worn to the Inception Ball the night I'd finally admitted my feelings for her.

As if she'd heard my silent gasp, she turned toward me and made a beckoning motion with one hand.

Fighting tears and the urge to grin like a fool, I made my way through the crowd toward the raised platform where Abigail Byler sat facing her new subjects.

It was hard work not to kiss her or reach for her as I went to stand beside her throne, taking my place as captain of her personal guard. That might be all I could ever be to her, but I knew in my gut *this* was right.

It was the best thing for the vampire race—the only solution—and if I had to stand by while Abbi took a succession of Bloodbound lovers, I would have to just suck it up and get through it.

Somehow.

Another problem for another day. Focus on keeping Abbi safe.

She walked to the front of the platform and quieted the assembly with a hand gesture, surveying the sea of vampires staring back at her with a combination of confusion and surprise evident on their faces.

Naturally, they'd expected to see Imogen before them, as usual.

"Thank you," Abbi said. "Thank you everyone for your attention. For those of you who don't know me, I'm Abigail Byler... Imogen's daughter. I have some news to share with you, and many of you will find it quite shocking. Imogen is... no longer with us."

There was a swell of sound in the cavern as people made exclamations of surprise and asked each other what was going on. I was wondering the same thing, but I strove to maintain a stoic expression.

Abbi pressed down on the air in front of her, settling them. "I know you have questions, and I will do my best to answer them. I want you to know, first, that everything is going to be okay. The Bastion will be okay, and so will you."

"Where did she go?" someone yelled. "Is she coming back?"

Abbi rolled her lips inward then out again, drawing a deep breath. "I guess I didn't make it clear. I'm very sorry but... Imogen is dead."

What? Shock rocked me back on my heels.

"The humans did it! They killed her," one of the Bloodbound shouted.

"We have to fight back," someone else yelled.

Growls and hisses filled the air, and Abbi raised her voice to be heard. "She was not killed by humans. Imogen died of natural causes."

"That's impossible," a woman near the front cried. "She's a vampire."

"It *is* possible," Abbi said. "If you'll give me a minute, I'll explain in as much detail as I can."

She glanced to her other side where Kannon stood guard, and he gave her a quick head shake as if to say, "No." What the hell had happened while I was gone?

Abbi continued anyway. "I'm going to be as honest as I can and give you all the information we have right now. To explain it properly, I first need to share another piece of news that might shock you... there is a cure for vampirism. Imogen took it. She became human again, and she died of old age shortly afterward."

Now the auditorium filled with murmurs. The vampires around the room turned to one another with stunned expressions.

Abbi had wisely left out the small detail that Imogen hadn't taken the cure voluntarily, that Larkin had surprised her by injecting her at the feast.

That information would probably not have gone over well.

"Obviously, the formula is not a viable cure for all vampires," Abbi continued. "Not yet. It isn't suitable for those who turned centuries ago or even many decades ago. It might also be deadly to those who turned after catastrophic injuries, like me. We just don't know yet. More research is needed and will get underway immediately."

Now I understood Kannon's warning expression. Total

honesty was Abbi's natural instinct, but it might have been the wrong choice in this particular situation. I sensed a shift in the room and not necessarily in a good direction.

The Bloodbound soldier who'd yelled before stepped forward. "What are you not telling us? Imogen would never have taken a 'cure' *if* such a thing even exists."

The guy's name was Chase. He was a former boxer from Las Vegas, and while his strength was an asset, we'd had a few disciplinary issues with him. He was like one of those guys who comes in as an intern and thinks he should be promoted to CEO the next week.

Honestly, if the ranks hadn't been dwindling, we might have kicked him off the squad for insubordination.

Both Kannon and I moved in his direction, but Abbi stayed us with a raised hand and remained unruffled. She actually smiled at him.

"All questions are welcome here. And you are welcome to visit the research lab we're setting up. The scientist who created the cure is actually here in the Bastion. Maybe we'll hold a series of informational meetings with her so anyone who wants to can ask questions."

"We don't need a talk show—we want to see Imogen," Chase insisted.

"Of course. Of course we'll have a memorial service for her, and if you'd like to view her remains, I can arrange it so her body lies in state. Anyone who wishes to will have the opportunity to come and pay their final respects."

That took some of the wind out of the guy's sails, and he shut up—at least for the moment. Abbi turned her attention back to the crowd at large.

"I know some of you have no interest in a cure, and that's fine. But others might. Some may have been turned against their will—or perhaps turned then regretted it later. *This* is why research is being done on a cure. I want to assure you, no one will ever be coerced to take it. And no one will be forced to participate in the studies. We're looking for *volunteers*. Every citizen of the Bastion is free to come and go as they choose. The days of vampires being compelled by force to do things they don't want to do are over."

"Tell that to the humans," Chase said, none too quietly. "We're as good as sitting ducks here with the little princess's Kumbaya crap."

Now I did move toward him. "Show some respect for your queen," I ordered.

"This isn't a queen," he yelled back. "This is a little girl! How is she going to lead us? Who's going to protect us from the humans now?"

Thankfully some of the other Bloodbound backed me up, cornering Chase and essentially driving him from the communal gathering space. But I was worried the damage had already been done.

He'd probably succeeded in planting doubt in more than a few minds. Abbi would have some work to do to gain the trust and respect of the citizens here. They weren't used to a Sadie-like approach, and I was afraid a lot of them would read it as weakness.

Abbi went to the front of the stage again to address the assembly. What they couldn't see—I hoped—was the trembling in her hands and top lip.

"Thank you all for coming today," she said. "I know it's been an enormous shock and you have a lot of new information to process. The memorial service for Imogen will take place in two night's time. You'll all receive more details about it tomorrow night as well as information about participating in the medical trials for the cure."

Then she turned and walked slowly toward the rear exit that led to her private quarters. As well as I knew her, I could tell she'd have preferred to run.

"You good here?" I asked Kannon. At his affirmative nod, I followed Abbi.

She'd done as well as could be expected from someone with no public speaking experience who'd been suddenly thrust into a role she wasn't prepared for and didn't really want.

I only hoped it had been good *enough* and there wouldn't be *more* Chases to deal with in the coming days.

6

———○———

NOT ALONE

Abbi

My knees wobbled as I left the Grand Dome, hurrying toward my chambers.

The trembling in my stomach made me feel like I might lose my lunch—if I had eaten any, which of course I hadn't.

What a mess. I had totally botched my first speech to the Bastion's people.

When Reece had stepped up beside me and defended me against that angry Bloodbound soldier, it had taken everything in me not to launch myself at him in gratitude.

And love. He still had my back, and it looked like I was going to need that support more than ever.

Now I saw what Kannon was talking about when he'd suggested—strongly—that I start giving the Bloodbound my queensblood in their rations. It looked like if I didn't, we'd have a mutiny before long. Maybe one was already in the works.

"Are you okay?"

I turned around to see Reece had followed me from the

Grand Dome and was now on the threshold of my private receiving room.

Running to him, I threw my arms around his neck and pressed my face against his throat. "I'm so glad you're back. I wanted to tell you about Imogen before I told the whole Bastion, but I couldn't wait. With the clinic staff members knowing and some of the Bloodbound knowing already, I was afraid word would get out and spread, and a panic might start. I think it might be too late."

"You did a great job keeping calm and showing everyone you're in control," he assured me.

I pulled back so our eyes could connect. His revealed no falseness, but I knew he was wrong.

"I didn't do a great job at all. I wanted to approach this like Sadie would, with honesty and transparency, but I think I might have made things worse by sharing all the details."

"I don't think it was bad to give them information... but it might benefit you to display a few Imogen-like qualities as well, to be a little... intimidating."

A simmer of nerves began in my belly. "What are you saying? You don't want me to order the execution of that soldier, do you? He's just afraid, and he was right—Imogen didn't take the cure voluntarily. And I'm not sure I *can* lead and protect everyone. You *know* I can't order someone's death."

Reece's eyes softened and he pulled me against his chest. "I know. My kind-hearted girl. You've probably already forgiven him. We'll just banish him."

That seemed awful too. As Eudora had pointed out, the outside world was becoming less hospitable to vampires every day.

"Where will he go?"

"I don't know, but we can't let him stay," Reece said. "Fear is like a cancerous tumor—if you don't remove it, it'll keep growing and infect the rest of the body. We can't let Chase go around spreading dissent and calling your capability into question."

I sagged against his strength, suddenly very tired. "Oh Reece, how did we get here? *How* am I supposed to do this?"

"One day at a time. You'll figure it out," he said as he ran one large hand over the back of my head and down my spine. "I'm afraid you *are* going to have to dose the Bloodbound with your queensblood though—and soon. We can't afford to lose anybody else at a time like this."

"I guess you're right. I don't like it though."

Pressing a kiss to the top of my head, he wrapped his arms around me more tightly. "I know, and believe me, I don't exactly love the idea of other soldiers sharing your blood—or your bed. But I'm not sure what the alternative is."

Suddenly struck by an idea, I lifted my head. "They're *already* loyal to you. I've seen it. They respect you. They listen to you. And you're Imogen's child too. I bet you'd have done a much better job with that introductory speech than I did, Mr. Debate Team President."

Reece gave me a chiding glance softened by a smile. "If you're trying to foist that sparkly crown onto my head, you can stop right there. I assure you... it won't fit. I don't have the necessary pheromones. As far as I know, vampires have never been led by a male. Besides, it's not just the loyalty factor. The queensblood also enhances the fertility of the drones."

The last sentence was delivered with a surly snarl.

"You know I don't want any part of that," I told him.

"I know, but if you *don't* procreate, that could be the end of our species. And before you say that it's meant to be, that the cure is the answer, there has to *be* one that works for *all* vampires. Who knows if Larkin can actually come up with one that'll work for everybody? Even if she does, not all vampires will choose to take it. Those who remain will *need* a queen. Without one, they'll be helpless, they'll be victimized. Either that or they'll fight back and be so weak they're sure to be wiped out entirely."

My exhale was a long sigh. "I'm just so afraid I'm going to mess everything up. And I don't know how to stop being afraid."

"Maybe the question isn't how to get rid of your fear," Reece said. "Maybe it's more a matter of being willing to do what you have to do—even though you *are* still afraid."

He stroked my cheek so tenderly it brought tears to my eyes. "I wish I could take this burden from you and do it for you. Unfortunately I can't. But I *am* here with you, no matter what. With or without the queensblood, you'll always have my loyalty."

Pulling slightly away, I lifted onto my toes to reach his mouth. "Thank you. I literally don't know what I'd do without you."

"You'll never have to find out."

A knock at the door startled us apart. Reece went to answer it. Kannon stood on the other side—and he wasn't alone.

My heart leapt, and my eyes flew open wide at the sight of the people who stood with him.

7

THE BOX

Abbi

"I'm sorry to disturb you," Kannon said, shooting Reece a quick side glance and an unspoken but very visible apology. "They said it was imperative to speak to you. They said you know each other?"

"Yes. Yes, we do. Please come in, everyone." I gestured for the group of four vampires to enter the receiving room at the front of my chambers.

Turning to Reece, I explained, "They're from the VHC. We worked together in Los Angeles."

"Queen Abigail. Thank you for seeing us," one of the older male vampires said, and they all bowed low.

I hurried toward them, arms open wide. "Please... please don't do that. We're all friends here. Please, everyone have a seat."

When my former co-workers were all seated on one of the two long upholstered red settees, I sat down on the other. "Wow, is it good to see you. I wasn't even sure you were alive. Is this everyone? Don't tell me the rest perished in the bombing?"

I knew the surviving members of the VHC had scattered after the terrorist attack. Sadie and Larkin had fled to Canada where they'd set up a lab. I assumed the others had gone into hiding since I hadn't seen or heard any evidence of them since.

No doubt Sadie's assassination had given them further motivation to stay out of sight.

A woman I recognized as a board member answered for the group. "There are others of us who made it... a few anyway. These are dangerous times, and not everyone left a forwarding address or wanted to risk coming here. But we were looking for you and thought you might have returned to the Bastion."

My head jerked back. "You were looking for *me*?"

Larkin had told me Sadie was disturbed by my disappearance and had tried to find out what happened to me, but why would the other members have been looking for me?

A man I'd seen around the VHC headquarters had a box in his lap. He held it out toward me, and Kannon quickly stepped forward to intercept it.

"If I may, my queen?" he asked with a raised brow.

I nodded and he lifted the lid, inspecting the contents before handing the box to me.

"Sadie left it with instructions that only you should open it," the older woman explained. "She called you our 'last hope.' I guess now we understand what she meant by it. We thought she meant for you to take over leadership of the VHC—we didn't realize you'd also become queen of the vampires. Not until we saw you up on that platform tonight."

It was hard not to cringe at the title, though I guessed it was technically correct.

"It's a... recent development. Thank you for bringing this to me. I'll open it later. Right now, I want to hear about you.

How did you manage to get here safely? Is the work of the VHC still going on or did you have to put everything on hold?"

They took turns answering my questions, each of them speaking in reverent tones that gave me major imposter syndrome.

Over the course of our conversation, I shared news of the cure with them—and its current drawbacks—and learned that one of the visiting party, a young man named Nolan, was a scientist like Larkin.

In fact, they knew each other.

"We worked closely together in Los Angeles. I'm thrilled to know she's here, and I'd be honored to help her set up a new lab," he said. "I know several other vampire scientists who'd be excited to join us in our work—if I have your permission to reach out to them and invite them to the Bastion."

"Of course. That would be great. This place is open to all vampires who want or need to come here," I assured him.

Just to one side of me, Kannon shifted from one foot to the other and huffed an irritated sounding breath. He must have been questioning the wisdom of my open-door policy.

Or maybe he was just getting tired of standing there, though he was the one who'd insisted on staying to protect me.

I'd give him something better to do. We were about finished here anyway. I stood, and everyone in the room rose to their feet as well.

"Thank you so much for coming and delivering this to me." I gestured toward the package. "It's especially precious to me now that we've lost Sadie. You're all welcome to stay here at the Bastion as long as you like or leave whenever it suits you. I look forward to working with those who choose to stay and carry on the work of the VHC. I know my friends Kelly and Heather will want to help. And Nolan, Kannon will find someone to escort you to Larkin right away. I'm sure she'll be delighted to see you."

Kannon smirked. "I'll 'escort' him myself. I'd hate for city-boy here to get lost in the caverns."

Reece left as well with the mission of finding a suitable cavern space for a new VHC headquarters and to let Kelly and Heather know about the latest developments so they could help.

That left me alone with all that remained of my beloved mentor.

ONCE INSIDE MY PRIVATE BEDCHAMBER, I set the box on my bedside table and removed its lid. Inside were a journal, a flash drive, and a sealed envelope. I decided to open the letter first.

My hands shook a little as I spotted Sadie's familiar, neat script. The letter was addressed to me personally.

DEAR ABBI,

If you're reading this, it means one of our friends found you before I managed to. I started searching for you and your housemates the first day you didn't report for work. I hope you are safe and healthy now, wherever this letter finds you. Unfortunately I had to make the difficult choice of fleeing the country. I will return as soon as possible, but for now I am running what's left of our heroic organization from abroad.

By now you know of the VHC headquarters bombing. What you may or may not know is that President Parker is responsible. His operatives continue to hunt me, which is why I had to leave and go into hiding.

As you know, I've always believed in diplomacy. Graham Parker is the single biggest challenge I've ever seen to my belief that peace and goodwill always triumph over evil eventually. I fear I made a critical mistake with him, by tipping my hand in a phone call to him shortly before the bombing. The lives lost in the explosion are most likely on my hands.

The flash drive you have received with this letter contains damning evidence against the president. It's likely that destroying it was the primary goal of the VHC attack. Of course, if I had died as a side effect, Parker would have been doubly pleased.

Luckily, we had a backup copy, the one now in your possession. Use it wisely. I know that you will, though I am plagued with guilt for giving it to you. Have no doubt —you will be his next target if you choose to take up the mission I leave behind.

I hate to put you in that position, and yet, I feel I have no choice. You are the last remaining hope for our people.

I know that you will rise to the occasion. Whatever happens, you cannot allow Imogen—or someone like her —to become the sole voice for the vampire species.

I never loved being a vampire, and yet I love our people. Because that's what we are, ultimately. Our livers may no longer function, our skin may not be able to tolerate daylight, and we may have extended lifespans, but when all is said and done, we are what we were at birth... people. And all people deserve to be safe and treated with dignity.

That is why you must be the one to lead our species instead of Imogen. Read the journal, and you will see why.

I regret that I never had the pleasure of seeing your

sweet face again. You truly are the daughter I always wished for and never had. Now you are the last and best hope of the vampire race. May God keep you and give you strength.

With love,

Sadie

By the time I finished reading, my eyes overflowed with tears. I swiped at them with my sleeve and lifted the journal, settling onto the bed with it on my lap.

Though it was old, the book was meticulously preserved. The handwriting inside matched the letter.

I started reading and let Sadie's words transport me back in time.

8

———

SADIE

1835 Hampshire

Tonight should have been one of the happiest of my life. I was, at long last, to meet the man I'd marry. Instead, Imogen made this occasion, like everything else, about *her*.

I pleaded with her not to wear the red dress and to let Lily pin her hair up in a proper style, but she simply laughed and tossed her long locks.

"Why? Are you afraid the prince will notice me instead of you? Even though you're the eldest and more 'marriageable?'"

"Father shouldn't have said that. And of course I'm not worried about the prince. I'm thinking only of you and your reputation."

"I don't need another mother, thank you. One is quite enough," Imogen said. "And she has fled the country and left us to fend for ourselves. So that's exactly what I'm going to do."

Then she flounced down the grand staircase and toward the ballroom like one of the peacocks that strutted about the manor's grounds.

Naturally, every eye in the room turned to her when she entered. When Father spotted her, his face flushed as red as the silk fabric she wore. I went to his side and slipped one gloved hand through his bent arm, encouraging him to take a stroll around the room with me and smile for our guests.

"It is a scandal," he hissed under his thick mustache. "She must go upstairs and change at once."

"It is too late," I told him. "People have seen her now. There is nothing to do for it but smile indulgently and mention throughout the night that she will do anything and everything possible to make our guests comfortable... including dressing like them."

At that, both our gazes went to the refreshment table where Prince Alexandru stood with his female companions. They conversed with those arriving at the table to make small plates or refresh their drinks but did not appear to be partaking of the refreshments themselves.

"I suppose after one more turn about the room, you should take me to meet the prince and his sisters," I said.

Father harrumphed. "They are a scandal as well. Those are *not* his sisters. They're his daughters—or at least that's what he claims."

"How is that possible? They look to be of the same age as the man."

One of Father's bushy eyebrows lifted sardonically. "They certainly do. As you know, our situation is dire, but I am considering withdrawing from the gentleman's agreement I made with him a few days ago. At least English nobility *pretends* at fidelity when out in society. I will not have you publicly shamed by a blatant philanderer."

My gaze returned to our guests before I purposely averted it in a heroic effort not to stare.

Sheltered though I was, I knew what "philandering"

meant. But *three* ladies at once? Was any man so bold? And were any women so tolerant? It didn't seem feasible.

"Perhaps the prince is telling the truth about their identities," I said. "Perhaps he is simply... *well preserved.*"

In spite of my attempt to be cheerful, I couldn't help but feel some disappointment. I had known it was too good to be true when Father guessed my suitor's age to be twenty-five.

Still... he *was* remarkably attractive. And I couldn't help but notice his gaze flickering in my direction every few minutes. Did he find me attractive as well? Or was he simply curious?

"Curiosity" couldn't begin to describe the state of my mind. I'd never been so eager to meet someone in my life. Here was a man for whom my family's debt was not an issue —a prince, no less.

For the first time in years, I had an actual chance of becoming a wife and mother.

My hopes rose even more when we were introduced. He took my hand and brought his lips lightly to my gloved knuckles as his extraordinary eyes stayed locked with mine.

"Enchanted," he said with a perfect English accent.

For a moment I was unable to respond. Those eyes. They were mesmerizing, the color of violets. His daughters shared the striking trait.

"Likewise. Your English is excellent, Prince Alexandru. Do you spend much time in London?"

"Not as much as I'd like, I'm afraid. I was educated in London though, and I do like to come back and visit whenever possible. Now I have found the *perfect* excuse."

He gave me a rakish smile before introducing the ladies who never strayed far from his side. "May I present my daughters? Katriona, Maria, and Daria. They do not speak English but have bade me to tell you how very lovely they find your home and how appreciative they are of your hospitality."

"Wonderful. I'm so happy you're enjoying yourselves," I said to them, though I wasn't sure if they even understood the words. Surprisingly, they didn't return my smile, just stood looking sullen. Perhaps they were hungry?

I gestured toward the table laden with food and crystal wine glasses. "Please, feel free to enjoy the refreshments."

"We ate just before arriving," the prince assured me. "One must keep one's energy up for dancing. Would you do me the honor?"

For some reason I blushed. I had danced with many men, young and old during the season in London.

But then I had known, in spite of my parents' hopes, that none of those dances would lead to a proposal. A girl can tell when a man is being polite and when he's interested.

This one was interested.

Placing my hand into his outstretched one, I said, "Thank you. I would love to," and allowed him to lead me out onto the parquet floor.

He was an accomplished dancer, and as we spun around the ballroom, I felt as if I was in a dream.

"You dance exceptionally well, my lady," he said, giving me another dazzling smile.

"It is you who are an exceptional dancer. If I have any skill, it is only because I have so much practice. Being on the marriage market for two years gives one ample opportunity to attend balls."

Prince Alexandru gave me a smoldering look and spoke in a slightly threatening tone. "If *I* had come to London two years ago, you wouldn't have lasted on the market two minutes."

Thankfully, he spun me away at that moment because my

face had heated until it was no doubt as red as the roses expertly arranged in vases around the room. To save money, they had been cut from our own property today instead of brought in from London hot houses.

No one seemed to notice. The attendees all seemed to be having a good time. Well, everyone but Imogen.

I had seen her dancing with one gentleman earlier—the elderly duke Mother recommended so highly—and so frequently. But now Imogen sat alone on a velvet bench set into one of the wall niches.

It was an area usually frequented by wallflowers—the girls no one asked for a dance—and she did indeed resemble a very large, very unhappy rose at the moment.

Turning away from the sight of her sulking, I renewed my determination to have a good time tonight.

It was her own fault she'd chosen to dress as the personification of lust. I had tried to warn her that the respectable young men in attendance would no doubt wish to take her on a private stroll in the dark gardens away from the public eye, but they wouldn't dare to dance with her in front of their mamas—not more than once anyway.

Over the course of the evening, Prince Alexandru danced with me three times, which was the maximum allowed by the rules of polite society. No one had ever shown such open interest in me. He complimented my dress, my hair, my smile. He laughed at even my weakest attempts at humor.

Each time he did, I was enthralled by the sound of his voice, the whiteness of his straight, even teeth, and the fullness of his lips. He was absolutely captivating.

What would it be like to be kissed by him?

Though she was two years younger, Imogen was much more experienced than I was at kissing. At least she had *done* it—many times, based on how she behaved with Will. I'd never kissed a man, but I wondered if tonight might be the night it finally happened.

Unfortunately a stroll in the relative privacy of the courtyard was out of the question because it had started raining.

Prince Alexandru did ask for a fourth dance, but I had to regretfully decline.

"You may not realize it, but in this country, more than three dances with the same partner is positively scandalous," I told him.

His spectacular eyes sparkled with amusement. "Far be it from me to cause a scandal. Perhaps I could escort you to the refreshment room instead?"

Though I sorely wished to accept his offer, my gaze drifted back to my little sister, who now wore the sullen pout of a scolded five-year-old.

Placing my hand lightly on his arm, I said, "I wonder, Prince Alexandru—"

"Just Alexandru," he corrected with a smile. "Please."

Blushing once again, I returned his smile. "Alexandru... I wonder if you might consider asking my sister for a dance."

His face quirked in confusion. "You want me to dance with your sister?"

"Well, look at her."

He turned to follow my line of sight to the corner where Imogen sat alone. He lifted one dark brow. "It's hard to miss her."

The tone of his remark worried me slightly, but he was right. She had made a spectacle of herself. Still, she was my sister, and I had never been able to stand seeing her unhappy.

"She can be mule-headed at times, but there is much to recommend about her, and for what it's worth, I believe she was motivated—at least in part—by a desire to make your daughters feel at home here. Everyone at the ball is so entranced by you, I think it would do a world of good if you danced with her and showed approval of her... *unconventional* appearance."

Alexandru's spellbinding violet gaze swung back around to meet mine. "Entranced, are they? The only one I want to entrance... is you."

He lifted my hand and kissed it again. "But I will dance with your sister if it makes you happy. After all, it is my hope that someday soon we'll be one big, happy family."

After a swift bow in my direction, he straightened, turned, and walked directly to Imogen.

Did he intend to propose then? It certainly sounded like it. My dancing slippers were practically levitating above the floor, and my heart felt as if it would pound straight through my chest.

That heady feeling did not last long. Within minutes it was apparent I was not the only one enchanted by Alexandru's chivalrous manners and striking looks.

As they turned about the dance floor, Imogen and Alexandru conversed and laughed. The way she stared up into his eyes reminded me of that terrifyingly beautiful cobra we had seen hypnotized by a snake charmer on our tour of India.

Of course we learned the snakes who danced in those shows later died a slow and painful death. I felt sorry for them.

My sympathy for Imogen diminished rapidly as the song went on. She had never seemed more like a cold-blooded reptile than she did to me in that moment.

Standing on tiptoe to whisper something into Alexandru's ear, she pressed her bosom against his arm and upper chest then pretended to lose her balance so he'd be obliged to grab her around the waist to keep her from "falling."

And when the dance ended? She pulled him toward the side entrance of the ballroom toward the French doors that opened to the courtyard and the formal gardens beyond it.

Letting my eyes follow their progress, I realized the rain had stopped.

57

9

NOT WHILE I LIVE

Abbi

At nearly dawn, Reece knocked on the door then entered.

"I think I've found a great spot for the VHC to set up shop."

Coming to my bedside, he asked, "What are you reading?"

"It's Sadie's journal. It was in the box. I'm starting to understand where it all went wrong between her and Imogen."

Closing the book, I set it aside, picking up the letter. "This is of more immediate concern. It's a letter from Sadie to me."

Reece lifted his brows and blew out a breath, taking the offered letter and unfolding it. "When did she write it?"

"After the bombing, before she fled to Canada. She left all these things for me, specifically. She called me the 'last, best hope' of the vampire people."

"That's what I've been saying." Reece smiled. "If only *someone* would listen."

I couldn't return his teasing smile. "There's more. She also gave me a flash drive. She said it contains evidence that will destroy Graham Parker."

"That's fantastic."

"I'm not finished. Sadie also said... well, she warned me."

Reece's smile vanished. "Of what?"

"She said Parker was definitely behind the VHC bombing, that he was after her... and that I would be his next target if I chose to take up where she left off and continue her mission."

"So don't. Parker never has to know where you are or *who* you are. Let the VHC people handle any sort of public awareness efforts or legal battles. You can stay here out of sight, where you're safe."

Reece's tone indicated he thought it was a done deal. An easy choice.

"What about the vampires who aren't here at the Bastion?" I picked up the flash drive and looked at it, then held it out toward him. "What about the evidence against the president?"

He took the device and rolled it around in his palm. "What's on this thing anyway? What kind of evidence are we talking about?"

"I don't know. I haven't had a chance to look at it yet."

Getting out of bed, I walked across the room to my laptop, which sat atop a desk carved from the cavern's natural limestone. Reece handed me the flash drive, and I inserted it.

A page came up asking for a password.

"It's encrypted," he said from over my shoulder. "Did she give you a password?"

I looked at the letter again, then checked inside the box, searching for anything that might be a password. Nothing looked likely. We tried Sadie's name, her birthdate, even a couple of phrases from the letter. Nothing worked.

"Why would she give you a flash drive you couldn't open?" Reece wondered aloud.

I shrugged. "Maybe she expected to still be around to give

me the password herself. Or maybe she felt the most important thing was keeping the data away from the wrong eyes. I don't know. Is there anyone you know of here who can hack into something like this?"

"I'll check into it tonight first thing. We'll find someone. In the meantime, we should put this drive somewhere safe—and keep you far from the public eye... maybe even here in your chambers under guard."

Though his suggestion was ridiculous, his desire to protect me was endearing. "Aren't you the one who said I need to start leading my people?"

"At the moment I'm most concerned about *your* safety," Reece said. His brows dropped low, giving him a glowering appearance. "I thought being queen would make you *safer*—you'd be guarded at all times, you'd have the loyalty of your people. I never thought it would put you in *more* danger."

"I guess every position of visible leadership carries with it some risk. The more you stick your neck out, the greater the chance an ax will fall on it."

Reece frowned, clearly disliking my choice of words. Stepping close, he encircled my neck with his large hands and met my gaze with fierce intensity.

"That will never happen to you. Not while I live."

Stroking the underside of my chin with his thumbs, he tilted my face up for his kiss. As always when he kissed me, it was like my brain and body disconnected. Emotion and sensation took over.

The taste of him, the possessive, greedy grip of his hands, the feel of his powerful body pressing against mine stole my breath and tempted me to forget the bizarre, life-changing events of this night and spend the daytime hours wrapped up in him, to forgo sleep altogether and dive headfirst into the sensual escape he offered.

But I couldn't.

For one thing, I was exhausted. For another, the Bloodbound soldiers posted outside my door would know Reece hadn't left my chambers, and their enhanced hearing would tell them exactly *why*.

I broke the kiss and stepped back. "As much as I'd love to spend twenty-four-seven, letting you 'guard' me, you should probably go so I can get some sleep. I have a full agenda tomorrow—starting with helping Larkin get everything she needs for her research."

He smirked. "I got the distinct impression that Nolan would be *more* than willing to give Larkin 'everything she needs.'"

"You noticed that too?" I laughed. "I also noticed that Kannon 'escorted' him from the room a little more forcefully than was necessary."

Reece gave me an alert glance. "You think he's attracted to her?"

"Don't you?"

"He says she drives him crazy. And he's not a fan of the whole cure idea—which is what she's all about. Besides, he's Bloodbound."

"So are you," I reminded him before pressing a lingering kiss to his full lips. "You're vampires, not machines. And he made his vow to Imogen, not to me. Imogen's dead."

Reece nodded. "That's a good point. You should have a ceremony when you give the Bloodbound your queensblood for the first time, give them the opportunity to publicly swear fealty."

"I'll think about it," I said.

"Good." He studied me. "It seems like maybe you're coming around to the whole idea of being queen."

"Well, seeing the VHC members today after so long reminded me of something. Sadie believed vampirism was the result of a cosmic mistake, that vampires should never have existed, and the species should be allowed to lapse into extinction. *But* she still devoted her entire life and all her energy into advocating for the ones who were here already. I can do that—or try my best to—at least until a universal cure makes it possible for everyone to become human again."

"You're still putting all your hope into that cure, aren't you?" Reece sounded disappointed.

"Honestly? Yes."

"I think it's a mistake."

"Well, at the moment, I don't have anything *else* to put my hope in. For a few minutes there, I thought there might be a hot vampire king who was going to take over and solve all my problems, but I guess he's not up for the job."

Reece laughed then his voice dropped into a lower register and became deliciously threatening. One of his dark eyebrows lifted. "Speaking of up for the job... there *is* one problem I can solve for you."

I feigned ignorance, but my breathing was quick and shallow as I backed away toward the bed and he prowled after me.

"Oh really? What's that?"

"You haven't been kissed *nearly* enough tonight," Reece said. "As one of your faithful drones, I *am* here to serve you."

Well... maybe *once* wouldn't hurt anything.

GRUMPY GUARD

Abbi

Emerging from the tight corridor leading to it, I stepped into the cavern housing the new offices of the Vampire-Human Coalition.

Kelly and Heather both looked up from their work and smiled at me. Everyone else bowed.

Even after three months, I still hadn't gotten used to it. Acknowledging the gesture of respect was the quickest way to get the vampire lawyers, paralegals, and other volunteers upright again, so I said, "Good evening everyone. Carry on."

The workers resumed whatever they'd been doing before my arrival, and I went to talk to my friends. At least *they* weren't bowing. Thank God.

"How are things going?" I asked, surveying the pile of burner phones spread across the table in front of them.

"Not bad," Heather answered. "I've learned a few new insulting terms for 'vampire.' Gotta love phone campaigns—people feel like they can say *anything* to you when you're not standing there in front of them."

Kelly laughed. "Yes, but there are a lot of nice people too.

In fact, I'd say it's about seventy-thirty, with the vampire-haters being in the minority."

"It's a *loud* minority." Heather raised a sardonic brow. "And rude. Don't they know our hearing is acute? They don't have to yell."

"Still, I like the sound of those numbers. What about the email and postal surveys?" I asked.

My friends were spearheading a human outreach effort, trying to gauge support for President Parker and his cronies versus support for vampire rights.

"Same breakdown," Heather reported. "At least on paper, people seem to think we should be allowed to have jobs and families and generally live our lives. Unfortunately *they're* not the people in charge right now."

I frowned. The new VHC was operating underground—literally and figuratively, keeping a low profile, as opposed to seeking media coverage as the organization had done under Sadie.

But we'd need to go public soon. It was important to keep communicating, to keep our plight in the public view and to show humans who we really were as opposed to letting President Parker and his narrowminded followers control the conversation.

The Bastion's population was growing larger by the day as more and more refugees streamed in, seeking shelter and protection from harsh new public policy efforts to drive them from their homes and jobs and generally make life as a vampire hell.

Of course President Parker was behind it all. He had to be stopped, but I wasn't sure how to do it.

No one had been able to decrypt the flash drive so far, so I still didn't know exactly what kind of evidence we had on him. It must have been bad—he'd ordered the bombing of the VHC to try to cover it up.

But I needed to know just *how* bad—and how much leverage I had to get him to back down on his aggressive anti-vampire rhetoric and policies *before* I requested a meeting with him.

"You don't happen to know any hackers, do you?" I asked my friends.

"There's a guy here who was a videogame designer," Kelly offered.

"Oh, I met this really cute guy in the Rainbow Cave the other night," Heather said. "He said he used to work for the Pentagon in IT before they instituted the federal vampire hiring freeze and he got laid off. Why? What do you need? Want him to screw up Parker's social media accounts?"

She grinned widely and wiggled her fingers in front of her like some sort of cartoonish villain. It was hard not to laugh at her enthusiasm for the idea.

"No. His people may be domestic terrorists, but we're not," I said. "I do have a tech problem though, and we need some help to solve it."

I hadn't told them about the flash drive—Sadie had said she hated to tell *me* about it because having it put a target on my back, but I was getting desperate.

"I need a flash drive decrypted. What was the IT guy's name?" I asked.

"I don't remember." Heather blushed. "But I do know where he lives—I went home with him that night. I definitely wouldn't mind seeing him again. Want me to let him know you'd like to talk to him?"

"That would be great."

Turning to Kelly, I asked, "How's *your* love life?"

"Non-existent. You know me, I'm a Bloodbound fangirl." She giggled then added in a teasing tone, "And they're not available because *someone* is monopolizing them."

"Believe me, I wish I could give them to you."

"All but one, right? How *is* Reece, by the way?" She gave me a silly eyebrow waggle.

Now I did laugh. Apparently our regular sleepovers—as in every night—were the worst kept secret at the Bastion.

"He's great. He and Kannon have been a huge help keeping those Bloodbound in line—in spite of the fact I'm *not* monopolizing them," I said. "Okay, gotta go. I need to stop by Larkin's lab and see how things are coming along."

On my way to the research lab, I veered into one of the caverns where construction was being done on new living quarters. With the vast influx of new residents, conditions were becoming a little tight inside the Bastion.

Though the cavern system had been mapped as far as five miles into the earth, only a small portion of it had ever been used for living space.

When this place had been a tourist attraction for humans, only the first few caverns past the opening had been explored. In the years since it had become a vampire habitat, there had been a good deal of expansion—sixty-four acres worth to be exact—but that was being stepped up exponentially now.

Workers were framing walls, installing plumbing and electrical lines. As I strolled through the expansion zone, the work crews stopped and bowed—once again giving me major imposter syndrome. But I went with it and acted the part because what else could I do?

It was a relief to get to the lab where once again I could be around someone who knew me for who I really was—just Abbi.

When I arrived, Larkin was bent over a sample, conversing closely with her research partner, Nolan. They were laughing about something.

"I had no idea science could be so funny," I said as I approached the worktable.

They simultaneously lifted their heads.

"Oh, Abbi—hi. I didn't hear you come in," Larkin said.

Nolan dipped his head. "My queen."

"How's it coming along?"

"Well, I'll put it this way. If we didn't laugh, we'd cry," Larkin said. "We keep running into the same problem. It works, the vampires revert to their human condition, and then not long afterward, they die—even the younger, healthier volunteers."

She literally wrung her hands in distress. "Which means we won't be having too many volunteers in the future. I mean, the ones who volunteered so far were so miserable as vampires they were willing to take the risk, but how many of those are there really? And how long can I go on in good conscience injecting people with a formula that most likely will end their lives? If I were testing a drug for humans, the trial would have been stopped already. I'm sorry. I know how much you're counting on this. I'm not sure what's going wrong. On paper it works. In real life it's a disaster."

"Don't worry. We'll figure it out." Nolan reached over and rubbed her shoulder. The contact wasn't lascivious—it was more a gesture of comfort—but he let his hand drift down to her back and linger there.

Hmmm. They'd been spending every night here together for weeks, but she hadn't mentioned any developing feelings between them to me. I wondered if she even realized how Nolan obviously felt about her.

Erasing any remaining doubt—in my mind at least—he added, "This lady can do anything she sets her brilliant mind to."

"Oh hush, you're the brilliant one," she argued, but I could tell from her expression she was pleased by his compliment.

A harumphing noise from my right drew my eyes to the

corner of the room. Kannon was there, wearing a look as dark as the shadow that had hid him from my notice earlier.

Because there was some controversy surrounding the necessity of a cure, we'd agreed a guard would be posted inside and outside the lab twenty-four seven. I was a little surprised to see Kannon here though. He was too high-ranking for a relatively menial job like this—and he didn't seem very happy to be here.

Maybe he'd had to fill in at the last minute for someone?

He stepped into the light. "My shift is up."

His announcement was aimed in Larkin's general direction, though he didn't make direct eye contact with her. "Tyrone will be here in a few minutes to replace me. My queen, I'll wait outside the lab for you—I need to speak with you, if you have time."

"Of course. I'll be out in a sec—I just dropped by for a quick update."

When he'd left the room, I turned back to Larkin with a quizzical glance.

"What's his problem?"

She shook her head rapidly and darted her eyes away. "I'm not sure."

The way her chest rose and fell in shallow breaths made me wonder if she knew more than she was letting on.

Seeming oblivious to his partner's abrupt change in body language and to Kannon's elevated position in the Bloodbound hierarchy, Nolan volunteered a guess.

"He's probably just mad his boss stuck him here guarding the 'boring science nerds.' He comes here every night, stands in that corner frowning like a gargoyle, and doesn't say a word aside from the occasional grunt."

Larkin's breaths grew even more audible, and her cheeks flushed a deep pink.

Interesting. Maybe Larkin wasn't aware of Nolan's attraction to her because she was attracted to someone *else.*

"Every night, you said?" I questioned Nolan. "That's unusual. The Bloodbound usually rotate shifts. I'll have to look into it."

"Don't bother. You've got enough to do as it is," Larkin said. "A grumpy guard is the least of our problems. Speaking of... Nolan, we should get back to work on this batch, or we're going to have to re-chill it and start again."

Instantly, his full attention was back on her.

Which I strongly suspected was the usual state of things in the lab—and the reason for Kannon's surly attitude.

NO WONDER

WHEN I MET Kannon in the corridor outside the lab, I decided to test my theory.

Keeping my tone nonchalant, I said, "Nolan certainly has a lot of confidence in Larkin."

Kannon's scowl returned. "That's not *all* he has a lot of."

"What does that mean?"

The big soldier's lips twisted to the side before he answered, "Nothing. It's just... he tells a lot of stupid jokes and stuff, trying to be *amusing*."

"What's wrong with that?"

"I don't know. Isn't science supposed to be all serious? I mean, they're literally dealing with life and death stuff in there. They should... focus."

I had to bite my own lip to keep from laughing at his obvious jealousy. "I think a little levity can be good —*especially* when you're dealing with life and death issues. They can't be serious every second. They'll die of stress before they find a cure."

His brows drew together. "They're vampires. They can't die of stress."

Now I laughed out loud. "I was being figurative. Listen, if his personality bothers you that much, you don't have to take shifts in the lab. I'm sure we can find someone else to do it."

Kannon's lips rolled in then out as he glanced over at the closed lab door.

"Nah. It's fine. I want to make sure sh—everyone is safe here. I don't exactly agree that we need a cure, but if other people want it, it's fine. I've seen a lot of vampires coming in here hoping it'll work, so I guess the idea does have some value. And anyway, I'm not letting what happened at the VHC happen here."

"Well, I appreciate it. I'm sure Larkin does too... although I know you two don't get along all that well either."

Kannon opened his mouth, but nothing came out. Then he shut it again and made a little sniff sound as he studied the cave wall beside us.

"Anyway..." he said. "That's not what I wanted to talk to you about. Have you located anyone who can get into that flash drive yet?"

"Not yet. I'm still putting out feelers. And new people arrive every night. As you know they fill out questionnaires about their job skills—eventually someone will show up who can decrypt the thing. Then I can make a plan to meet with Parker."

Kannon's expression turned stormy once more. "Why don't we just take him out? Say the word, and I'll put together a small strike team of our best guys. We could be ready to go in a matter of days."

"No. We are *not* going to assassinate the president of the United States. That's something Imogen would do, and as you may have noticed, I'm not Imogen."

He grinned. "I noticed. Maybe you should be a little *more* like her—at least when it comes to some things. We're losing

Bloodbound soldiers left and right to defection, and recruiting replacements is tough."

"Are you that mean of a commander?" I teased.

"Maybe, but that's not the reason. The troops are getting restless, you know? When it comes to the celibacy requirement, I mean. It was bad enough when we had to wait weeks or months for a turn with Imogen. But now... well... it hasn't gone without notice that the only one you ever invite to your chambers is Reece."

"I see."

He held up two hands in front of him in a defensive posture. "I'm not telling you what to do—you're queen. But maybe you should start getting a little scarier and take a few defectors' heads... show them what happens if they desert and take a mate. They're breaking the rules because they don't think you'll do it."

"They're right. I'm not going to execute someone for falling in love. I'd be the world's worst hypocrite."

"Well then, maybe, you know... spread the love around a little bit... give the troops some hope and invite a few of the Bloodbound to your chambers. Most of them are pretty eager for a turn with you."

His hands went higher. "Not me—I don't mean me. Reece would slit my throat in my bunk at the barracks. But the other guys... it would go a long way."

"Maybe it would," I said. "But it's not going to happen."

Kannon threw up his hands. "Well then, I don't know what to tell you, Abbi—I mean, my queen. If we can't get this flash drive open and get leverage on Parker and it *does* come to war, you're not going to have enough soldiers to even stand a chance."

"We'll have to put our faith in the flash drive evidence then—and in Larkin's cure."

"Yeah, okay," he muttered. "In the meantime, maybe you

could increase the amount of queensblood in our rations. I don't know if it's because you're younger than Imogen or what, but the current amount doesn't seem to be getting the job done."

"Can I tell you a secret? I haven't been putting it in at all."

Kannon's jaw dropped open so fast and so far, I thought it might hit the floor.

"It just didn't feel right to me to force loyalty," I said. "If I can't earn it, maybe I don't deserve it."

Now Kannon was shaking his head, and his eyes drifted back to the lab door. "No wonder," he said in a voice so low I wasn't sure he even meant to say it out loud.

I looked at the door too—the door behind which Larkin stood working oh so closely with her attractive male partner.

Acting on intuition and the desire to tease my old friend, I said, "Kannon... now that I think of it... maybe I *should* set an example. Can you give me the names of the Bloodbound who've violated those celibacy vows? And call a gathering in the Grand Dome?"

His eyes shot back to me and opened wide in alarm. Before I could tell him I was kidding, he excused himself.

"I need to get to... I've gotta go. Let me know if you change your mind about that strike on the White House."

Then he speed-walked away, nearly running into Reece, who was coming down the corridor.

1 2

ACTING MORE QUEENLY

It wasn't every day I saw a look like *that* on Kannon's face.

He was without a doubt the baddest of all the badass soldiers I'd worked with. Now he was practically sprinting down the hall away from Abbi, looking terrified.

I turned and watched his rapidly disappearing back. "What's going on with *him?*"

"I was wondering the same thing," Abbi said. "I think Larkin might know, but she's not talking either."

Picking up on the amusement in her voice, I studied Abbi's face. "Do you think those two are..."

"Wouldn't surprise me."

"And how would you feel about that?" I probed. Hopefully my tone didn't give away my jealousy.

As queen, Abbi had the right to spend time with any and all of her Bloodbound soldiers whenever she liked doing *whatever* she liked.

She'd assured me several times she had no interest in claiming carnal rights with the others, but it was tradition, and I knew a lot of the other guys were hoping for it—

especially now that their queen was a beautiful nineteen-year-old instead of a woman who'd walked the earth for more than two hundred years.

"Well, I love them both, so it makes perfect sense for them to love each other," Abbi said. "Anyway, it's their business."

While I felt the tension leave my body, another worry took its place. "Is it though? If they *are* involved and word gets out, it's not going to be good. The other Bloodbound will start feeling like they've got carte blanche to do the same—you'll have the inmates running the asylum here before long."

"Well Kannon had a very helpful suggestion about that," Abbi said.

I didn't understand the note of mischief in her voice. My own was full of trepidation. "Oh?"

"He thinks I should start inviting Bloodbound soldiers to my chambers to give the rest of them hope."

The tension snapped right back into place—and doubled. It was joined by a burning sensation in my stomach and an involuntary growl. I reached for Abbi, pulling her into my arms.

"The *only* Bloodbound who's setting foot over your threshold is standing right in front of you. If anyone else tries it, his *hope* better be that he can outrun me."

Abbi laughed and kissed me. Pulling back to meet my eyes, she ran her hands over my shoulders and down my chest. "Oh my. What a big, scary vampire you are."

The combination of her touch and the sexy tease in her voice lit me on fire. I looked up and down the corridor to make sure we were alone.

Then I backed her up against one wall and pressed the front of my body to hers.

Nuzzling her neck, I murmured, "I don't know about

scary... but yeah... if you want to discuss *size,* I'll be happy to escort 'my queen' back to her chambers."

Abbi laughed and ran her hands over my abdomen and around to my back to pull me even closer.

"I suppose as queen it's my prerogative to take a little 'private time' when I want to. Let's go."

A COUPLE HOURS LATER, Abbi moved to the edge of the bed and put her feet on the floor, shaking out her long hair.

I studied the beautiful curves of her waist, wanting more than anything to hook an arm around it and drag her back under the covers with me.

She *did* have responsibilities though, and so did I. Pity though it was, we couldn't spend all day in bed.

"Do you think we'd have wound up together if we hadn't been turned?" she asked, pulling on a silky dressing gown.

I folded my hands behind my head and grinned at her. "Absolutely. There's no way you would have been able to resist me. Especially when I kept showing up at your doorstep every day. Your father would have had to chase me off with a pitchfork—and I bet he has one of those."

She laughed. "He does. And several hunting rifles. But seriously... would you have pursued me?"

"Abbi... you were beautiful *before* the queensblood kicked in. And smart, and funny, and fascinating. Should I go on? I told you then, and I'm even more sure of it now—we were meant to be together. I think the universe has proved that quite spectacularly."

"And yet it's causing problems that I'm not 'spreading the love around,' as Kannon says."

Tension crept back into muscles that had been very, *very* relaxed. I didn't like the note of uncertainty in her voice.

"Have you changed your mind about that? Are you considering it now?"

"Noooooo." She dragged the word out, making it sound more like a "maybe" than a denial.

"I still don't want that. But I think you might have to stop sleeping over—just for a while," she added quickly. "We can't exactly keep what we're doing in here a secret—there are guards posted outside my door round the clock—guards with supernaturally acute hearing. As much as I hate it, I think I have to start acting more *queenly*. I can't keep making the other Bloodbound jealous and unhappy."

"So you're just going to make me jealous and unhappy," I quipped, though I was only semi-joking.

"Reece..."

Her tortured tone plagued me with instantaneous guilt.

Crawling to the edge of the bed where she stood, I wrapped my arms around her waist and pressed my forehead to her chest.

She sank her hands into my hair, rubbing my scalp in a soothing way.

"I get it," I grumbled. "I do. I don't like it, but I get it—and you're right. We can't afford to lose any more soldiers."

After pausing to draw a deep breath and letting it out on a long sigh, I said, "Do what you have to do... whatever that is."

Then I got up, dressed, and left her chambers, muttering to the guards who stood watch outside, "I hope you're happy."

I certainly wasn't.

13

LOST AND FOUND

Abbi

It was impossible to sleep.

The bed seemed too large without Reece in it, and I was cold. I got up and put on a robe then crawled back under the luxurious covers, dragging Sadie's journal into my lap from the bedside table.

Opening it to the page where I'd stopped last time, I resumed reading the words of my mentor, desperate for some wisdom—or at least some comfort.

Following her description of the ball in 1835 was an entry written two weeks later in Sadie's beautiful hand.

TODAY IS **the happiest day of my life. I am to be a bride! Alexandru is the most wonderful man. Following the ball, he courted me daily, arriving each night to walk with me in the gardens, take me for carriage rides, and escort me to the theater in London.**

His daughters accompanied us as chaperones, of course. They do not seem overly friendly, but I suspect it

is only a matter of the language barrier. While I am far too young to be viewed as a mother figure to them, I have high hopes that in time we shall all become fast friends.

Already I am learning more of their language, which is a good thing since we will be making our home in Moldavia where Alexandru owns a castle and extensive properties.

Because of his unusual sleep patterns, the wedding will take place tonight instead of at the traditional hour. I think a wedding ceremony by candlelight will be exquisite.

The only thing dulling my happiness is the absence of my sister. Imogen left Stony Hill Park the night after the ball without saying goodbye, going to join our mother on her holiday. I have not seen her since. Her letters said she was happy for me but would not return for the ceremony with Mother and our aunts. Her excuse was that she had not yet seen Rome and Venice.

It is clear she is angry that Father's arrangement with the prince was for me instead of her. I only hope it does not drive a wedge between us for the rest of our lives and that Imogen will someday find her own prince, figuratively speaking.

Though knowing her as I do, I am convinced she will find a way to make it literal and wear a crown of her own one day.

THE NEXT ENTRY described the wedding and party that followed in detail. There were several entries cataloguing their honeymoon trip, a tour of Europe, and then one describing the castle in Moldavia, which seemed to overwhelm Sadie with its size and opulence.

After that there was a gap of several decades before the next entry.

That's weird.

I flipped a few pages ahead and then back, sure I must have missed some. But no, the next entry was from 1869—more than thirty *years* later.

What had happened? Had Sadie become so busy she'd simply had no time to journal?

As I read on, the explanation wasn't spelled out exactly, but it was pretty obvious when you read between the lines—she'd learned the *reason* for her husband's unusual sleep patterns, and it had rocked her world off its axis.

ALEXANDRU CAME HOME COVERED in blood again. It is happening more and more often, and I suspect he "forgets" to wash before coming to our chambers just to torment me. Or to punish me.

He is convinced I have somehow willfully failed to conceive these past thirty-four years, though I have sworn to him on all I hold dear that I wanted nothing more than to be a mother and have his child.

Now I think perhaps it is for the best that I did not.

I am not certain it is even possible for one such as I— or that our particular sort of "family" should even exist.

When the prince bit me during our wedding trip and made me like him and his other "daughters," he assured me it was because he saw something special in me, because his people needed a true queen to survive and thrive.

In spite of my shock and horror upon learning his "people" were not the citizens of Moldavia, but a race of blood-drinkers, I have done my best to fill that role and to try to accept the more frightening and repulsive necessities of life as a night-dweller.

But the more time that passes without my giving Alexandru an heir, the angrier he becomes and the more violence he enacts against the humans here in Moldavia.

The servants talk of rumors spreading wild through the villages surrounding the castle. I fear we may need to vacate the area soon and find a new home somewhere far from here where no one knows who, or what, we are.

THE NEXT ENTRY was dated several years later in 1875. It was short but its tone was decidedly more optimistic.

THE DOCTOR HAS CONFIRMED what I have suspected for weeks now. I am with child! Alexandru will be over the moon when he returns from Paris and I tell him. I only hope it is soon.

Life here in San Francisco is strange, and it is lonely without him. I am hopeful we can return to London to raise our child. There are of course no friends or family left there, but at least the environs will be familiar, and the old estate in Hampshire was left to me when Mother and Father passed.

It was an idyllic place to grow up. I would love for my son or daughter to experience the same kind of childhood I had, or at least as close to it as possible without being able to frolic on the grounds of Stony Hill Park in the daylight.

How I wish I could watch a sunrise again and share the experience with my children! Life does not move in reverse, however, and I shall endeavor to move forward

with gratitude for this new life inside me and with hope
for the world at large.

SADIE HAD A CHILD? My heart raced with excitement and
hope of my own. If the baby had been a girl and I could find
her, *she* could take over the reigns as queen and lead our
people. It would be the perfect solution—especially as
Alexandru and Sadie's daughter was legitimate royalty—and
Sadie's direct, biological descendant.

My hopes were dashed when I read the next entry in the
journal.

I DEPART for Hampshire and Stony Hill Park today, but
contrary to my hopes and dreams, I will not be raising a
family there. When Alexandru returned from Paris, he
was not alone.

Imogen was with him.

As it turned out, the "business" that kept him in France
for such an extended time was my sister.

He'd encountered her in Paris at the French Crimson
court where she had finally found what she was looking
for in all her travels—a vampire who would agree to turn
her. In fact, she was the daughter of France's vampire
queen.

Alexandru walked into our home in San Francisco
with Imogen on his arm, boldly announced that after four
decades of marriage, he had realized his "error." He had
chosen the wrong sister.

As I stood gaping, he ordered our servants to move my
things from our shared room into the guest quarters and
informed me that I was welcome to stay, like the rest of

his former paramours, the women I had initially taken for his sisters the night we'd met.

I did not even tell him about the baby. Alas, whether from the shock or grief or the mysterious rules of vampire physiology, I lost the child.

Perhaps Imogen will be able to give Alexandru what I never could—an heir. Either way, I am now convinced the vampire race is a plague upon the earth. Certainly my husband is.

If I could go back to the night of the ball in Hampshire, I would refuse to dance with him or entertain the notion of the marriage. I would attempt to save my sister as well, but I suspect she would have disregarded my warnings, as she did this morning when my carriage arrived to take me to the port for my voyage to England.

"He cannot be trusted," I told her. "Eventually he will betray you as well."

She laughed. "I stopped trusting men the day our father sold you to a vampire. Do not worry about me, sister. Unlike you, I always put myself first. Alexandru needs a queen... but I do not *need* a king."

"What do you mean? Do you not love him then?" I asked.

"Love? I learned at age eighteen when Will died of scarlet fever that love is pointless. Power is what matters. And you should have seized power from Alexandru long ago. If he were capable of ruling the vampire species on his own, do you not think he would have done so? Instead, he has collected and discarded a succession of candidates, looking for a woman strong enough to prop him up and secure his shaky hold on the vampire race."

She shot me a wicked grin. "Well, he has found her— but I am no prop, as he will soon learn. I wish you a safe journey. We will meet again. And by then... I predict you

will have forgiven me and realized I am doing you, and our entire species, a favor."

"But how will you defy Alexandru?" I asked her. "He will not go easily, and he has amassed many followers."

Imogen only grinned in that cat-like manner of hers. "I have a few friends of my own, big sister. And they are loyal to me to the point of death. I call them the Bloodbound."

Wow. So that was how the feud between the sisters had started. Imogen had stolen Sadie's husband—and her royal title.

I wondered how long Alexandru and his daughters had survived once he'd married Imogen and made her queen. My bet was on not too long.

I'd have to read further when I had the chance, but for now I needed to get some sleep.

Tomorrow night was bound to be another long one, filled with duty and responsibility. I also had a big decision to make—whether to take Kannon's and Eudora's advice and begin influencing the Bloodbound, with my blood and my body, to continue serving loyally.

Or to simply let the defections continue and take the chance we'd never need an army to defend us in an all-out war between vampires and humans.

14

A MATTER OF SURVIVAL

Reece

Rolling out of my cold *single* bunk, I dressed in my uniform and headed for the door of my room in the Bloodbound barracks.

A dull headache throbbed in my temple, and I rubbed it in an attempt to soothe the pain.

If I'd been in Abbi's bed, no doubt I'd have gotten less sleep, but I bet I'd feel a hell of a lot better right now.

Sleeping alone again was not a welcome experience. It had been a week since I'd been invited to her chambers, and each day the feeling of deprivation grew worse.

Last night was particularly bad, with me tossing and turning and repeatedly drifting into dreams where I was with her then waking in disappointment over and over again.

Frankly, I felt like I'd been run over by a truck. Several times.

Kannon on the other hand, looked fresh as the proverbial daisy. He was in the corridor, waiting for me.

"Hey there brother. Time to rise and moon-shine. Ready for the troop inspection?"

His sunny grin and upbeat tone irritated me. "What's got *you* in such a good mood tonight?"

Kannon used to be as surly and cynical as I was. Lately though, he was acting like a goofy kid, in a good mood and joking around all the time.

"Nothing. Just high on life my friend," he said. "It's a great night to be alive—undead, whatever."

He laughed and slapped my back in a friendly way.

I responded with a not so friendly glare.

"What the hell is wrong with *you*?" Kannon asked. "You've been in a foul mood for the past week."

Dipping my chin and raising one brow, I gave him a loaded glance. "Hmmmm, let's see... what happened about a week ago? Oh, right. Someone told my woman to kick me out of her bed for appearance's sake. That same someone also suggested she start taking other lovers. With friends like you, who needs enemies?"

Kannon held up both hands in a surrender pose. "Sorry dude, I didn't make the rules. You wanted her to be queen— it's part of the job. Vampire life has its advantages, but it also has a few drawbacks."

I huffed a humorless laugh. "Yeah, a few. But Abbi doesn't want to claim her rights with the Bloodbound—and I'm certainly not going to pressure her to sleep with other guys."

"Fair enough. Fair enough. I can't say I blame you." Kannon shot me an apologetic half-grin. "But don't say I didn't warn you when the shit hits the fan and it's just you and me left to defend the place."

Despite his fatalistic words, I detected an unfamiliar bounce in Kannon's step as we walked together through the caverns toward the stairway to the surface. He smiled and greeted everyone we passed.

"Seriously. What is up with you lately? Why *are* you so damn happy all the time?" I asked.

"I told you. Life is good. We have a queen who doesn't torture us or kill people on a whim, we're protecting more vampires than ever, and there's a cure in development."

"I thought you didn't approve of the cure."

Kannon shrugged. "I'm coming around to it. I mean, it *is* voluntary, and I've seen the proof that a lot of vampires *do* want it. Just because I don't, doesn't mean it's a bad thing."

"That's quite a change of heart. Though I guess you *have* been spending a lot of time at Larkin's lab," I prodded.

Now he looked away, avoiding direct eye contact. Oh yeah—he was into Larkin. It took one to know one, and I *knew* what it was like.

"The work needs protection," he said in a casual tone.

"The work," I repeated with a chuckle then decided to have mercy on him and drop it. It wasn't smart to throw stones when my own house was made of the thinnest possible glass.

Reaching the surface, we surveyed the assembly of Bloodbound soldiers standing in formation in the meadow above the Bastion.

Moonlight shone down on them, gilding their armor and black leather uniforms and making them look like chess pieces made of polished onyx.

Other than Abbi's personal guard and a couple of teams who were out in the field on missions, the full contingent was there.

And there was a glaringly obvious problem.

Kannon and I exchanged troubled glances, clearly thinking the same thing—our numbers were *way* down. There had been far more defections than I'd even realized.

During her address to the full population, Abbi had told the Bastion's citizens they could come and go at will.

Far too many of the Bloodbound had taken her up on the offer.

Though she hadn't specifically mentioned the freedoms applied to her soldiers, she hadn't strictly forbidden them from leaving either. I knew she didn't want to force people to serve, but this was bad. We were vulnerable.

While I supervised troop exercises and training, Kannon checked in by radio with our teams out in the field. He approached me, holding out his walkie and wearing a look of concern.

"You need to hear this."

I took the device, speaking into it. "This is Reece. What's going on there?"

"Sir, we spotted them about twenty miles from the Bastion—ten Humvees—each of them with about five human troops aboard."

"Military?" I asked. "Or VSU?"

VSU was short for Vampire Suppression Unit. They were like SWAT teams, only they dealt exclusively with vampires and had specialized UV rounds and liquid platinum ammo. They were operated by local municipalities while the military of course was under federal control.

"Neither, sir," the commander said. "I've never seen a unit like this one. Could be something new?"

Kannon and I looked at each other. "Parker's been threatening to form his own personal tactical force," he said.

"I *really* hope that's not what this is. They are way too close for comfort."

Just the existence of the Bastion violated the terms of the Crimson Accord, which prohibited the assembly of more than ten vampires at a time in one location.

If Parker's personal strike force were to find the vampire sanctuary and stronghold, all its citizens could be sent to prison camps.

Abbi, who'd escaped from a prison camp and was now leading the Bastion, would be severely punished and probably in a highly public way.

I couldn't let that happen.

I lifted the walkie to my mouth again. "Did you get any surveillance footage?"

The device crackled to life as the field team commander answered. "Sure did. Bringing it back your way now."

About fifteen minutes later, the team returned, and the commander sought us out, handing over a tablet on which he'd captured video of the novel paramilitary unit.

Just as he'd said, their uniforms weren't Army, Navy, Marines, or Air Force, and they weren't SWAT or any other sort of police.

Zooming in on one of the soldiers, I studied the insignia on his shoulder patch. I tipped the pad toward Kannon. "Ever seen anything like this before?"

He snarled. "Only in documentaries about Nazi Germany. That looks a hell of a lot like a swastika."

"I thought so too, except instead of a circle with a bent-armed cross inside, it's two crossed P's."

His expression was grim. "P.P... President Parker? There's an American flag beneath the emblem."

I shook my head, rubbing my temples. "Damn. He did it—he created his own personal army. This is bad. This is really, really bad."

Turning back to the team commander, I asked, "Which way were they traveling?"

"They were headed toward Quicksburg."

"That's where the Shenandoah Caverns are," I said more to myself than to the others. "Someone's been talking. It's no accident they're in this area."

Kannon nodded. "I've been worried that Abbi's policy of

letting people come and go as they please might lead to discovery."

When I shot him a warning glance, he added, "Not that I'm questioning my queen. It's just something that occurred to me as a possibility. She's generous. She believes in personal freedoms. There's risks with that."

"Well, they'll find no vampires at Shenandoah," I said. "Unfortunately they'll probably keep checking the major caverns until they finally do hit the right location. The day is coming—sooner rather than later. We've got to be ready for it."

"Agreed. Which means we can't lose any more Bloodbound. We *can't* allow any more defections. It's a matter of survival now," Kannon said. "And as you're the queen's *closest* advisor—probably the only one she'll listen to —I think *you* should be the one to tell her."

"Tell her what?"

Though his expression was apologetic, his voice was firm.

"That it's time to pick a soldier... and invite him to her chambers."

15

A SURE THING

When Reece showed up at my door, I knew immediately something was very wrong.

He looked pale and nauseous, like he'd forced himself to eat five pounds of cooked liver—and vampires don't eat.

My stomach rolled, and my fingers and toes suddenly felt ice cold.

"What's going on? What happened?"

Reece swallowed hard. "I need to... talk to you. Can I come in?"

"Of course." I stepped back to make way for him, scanning him from head to toe. Had he been injured during training? "Are you okay?"

"Yes. I'm fine. There's just something important we need to discuss." His grimace contradicted his answer.

"Okay..."

Reece entered the room with dragging footsteps and collapsed onto the nearest of the two velvet-upholstered settees. I sat beside him, hands clasped tightly in my lap, rocking slightly as I waited.

For the longest time he didn't speak, just sat there, hunched over with his head drooped. When he finally lifted it, there was obvious pain in his eyes.

"It's time," he croaked.

"Time? Time for what?"

It appeared to take a monumental effort for Reece to explain. He drew a deep breath then let it out slowly.

"Abbi... you've got to... choose someone. You've got to choose one of the Bloodbound and invite him to your chambers—tonight. And you've got to give all of them your blood to drink. It's a matter of life and death now."

"What *happened*?" I repeated, reaching out and grasping his hand.

Whatever it was must have been bad for him to do such an about face on the matter. "Yesterday you were threatening to remove the head of anyone who touched me."

"Yesterday we didn't know about Parker's personal army— the army that's making its way *here*. As much as you don't want it to, it's going to come down to war, and we won't stand a chance if we don't have enough warriors. You have to do whatever it takes to retain our current troops and reinforce their loyalty."

"I'll give them my blood, okay? I'll do it. But I don't want to invite anyone to my bed. I don't want to be with anyone else that way. I can't believe you're asking me to."

"You think I want this?" he said, looking like he was at the edge of sanity. "I'd rather drink molten platinum. It's going to *kill* me. But better me than the whole population of the Bastion or the whole vampire race. Parker has to be stopped. Military force is the only way I know of to do it—and that means keeping the Bloodbound happy and loyal."

For a long time, I said nothing. This was a moment I'd prayed would never come.

But all the while I'd put my hopes on a cure for

vampirism or the impenetrable flash drive, this inevitability had been marching steadily closer.

Now it was here. I was out of time and choices.

"Okay." The word was a breath, a whisper.

Reece heard me loud and clear. His head snapped up, and his lilac eyes lasered to mine. "You'll do it?"

Feeling suddenly exhausted, I nodded. "Yes. Because *you're* asking me to. Who do I have to sleep with? How many?"

He swallowed several times as if trying to repress a surge of bile. "I've given it some thought. We'll post a schedule in the Bloodbound barracks—that way there won't be any fighting about whose turn it is, and the guys will all have hope that theirs is coming."

"So, all of them then."

He nodded morosely. "Eventually. The visits could be separated by a week—or two—I mean, there's no rush, we're immortal. The first one should happen immediately though, to prove you're being forthright about it."

"I guess if I have to do it, that's as good a plan as any. Who's first?"

"It *would* have been Chase, the soldier who shouted you down in your first speech to the people. He was next up in Imogen's rotation, which is probably a large part of the reason he was so angry she died."

Reece shifted on the settee and dragged his palms down the tops of his pant legs. "Now that he's banished, the next in line is Jason. He's young, a little older than us. Kind of rough around the edges but a good soldier. Considering you could have him executed if he displeases you, I'm pretty sure he'll be..."

Cringing, Reece went on, speaking through clenched teeth. "... gentle with you. If not, he'll be dealing with me."

I blinked. "But how would you... what are you planning to do—watch?"

His complexion darkened. "No, but I'll damn well be guarding the door to your chambers tonight."

"Oh Reece... don't torture yourself like that. You don't have to be there." With his enhanced senses, he'd be able to hear everything that went on in the room.

"Yes. I do," he vowed. "I want every sonofabitch who goes in there to have to see my face on the way in—and out."

THE KNOCK on my chamber door caused me to jump.

When I summoned Jason only minutes ago, I'd sort of hoped it would take him longer to make his way here. Maybe it was for the best—we'd get it done and over with quickly. It wasn't like I was going to get *less* nervous about this the longer it dragged on.

"Enter."

The door opened, and Jason stepped in. I recognized him as a soldier I'd seen around the Bastion, though we'd never officially met.

Now I knew what Reece had meant when he'd described him as rough around the edges. Both of his arms, as well as the top of his chest visible where the neckline of his uniform shirt parted, displayed tattoos.

Jason looked a little like Kannon, tall and blond, but he was leaner, wide-shouldered and muscular in a sinewy, less bulked up way. When I'd seen him before, he'd worn a reddish-blond beard trimmed in the Van Dyke style.

Tonight, he was clean shaven, which made him look younger and a tiny bit less intimidating.

If I hadn't been in love with Reece, I would have said

Jason was handsome. Well, I guessed he *was* handsome. It was just a fact.

He was a Bloodbound vampire after all. It had nothing to do with how I felt—or didn't feel—about him.

"Good evening, my queen." He bowed deeply. "You look beautiful tonight. You always do, but tonight you're especially lovely."

Flushing at the unexpected, *unwanted* compliment, I instructed him to rise. When he did, our eyes met. His shone with excitement and clear anticipation. Mine probably resembled the shell-shocked gaze of a deer mesmerized by the sudden appearance of headlights on a dark country road.

Okay, think. Settle down. You're the queen. You're in charge here.

Suddenly I wished I'd read Imogen's journals. They probably detailed this sort of encounter—which, *gross*—but at least I'd have had some clue about how to handle this.

As it was, I really had no idea what to do. Yes, I'd been with Reece, but that was making love as opposed to just sex, and he'd led the way in those interactions.

In this one, *I* was supposed to be the leader.

Should I just tell the guy to strip and get in the bed? The whole thing was horribly awkward.

Jason smiled. "Do you mind if I have a seat?"

"No, of course not." I let out a nervous laugh. "Forgive me for not offering. Would you like some wine or anything... else to drink?"

His gaze darted to my neck then rushed back to connect with my eyes again. "Maybe later. Maybe you'd like to sit too?"

While he sat in a chair, I lowered myself onto the edge of my bed, fiddling with my fingernails.

"I want to thank you for inviting me here," Jason said. "I'm happy for the chance to get to know you better."

The polite response would have been something along the lines of, "Yes, you too." But I didn't want to get to know him better—not in *this* way, anyway. Instead, I blurted the question at the top of my mind.

"How many times were you with Imogen?"

Jason gave me a rueful grin. "None, unfortunately—she was a stunning woman. See, I only came to the Bastion and joined the Bloodbound a year ago. My turn in the rotation hadn't come up yet. I was getting close, but then Imogen... well... allow me to say I'm *not* disappointed in how things worked out. You're already a better queen and far more beautiful."

The more compliments he gave me the more my stomach squirmed.

"The seduction act isn't necessary, you know. I've already summoned you here, and I intend to fulfill my queenly *duty*, so I'm kind of a sure thing."

Jason laughed. "It's not an act. I *do* find you beautiful—all the guys do."

His face and tone changed, becoming deadly serious. "I'm just the lucky bastard who gets to bed you first."

I almost argued that Reece had been the first. But that would have flown against the entire reason for this charade —to keep the other Bloodbound from being jealous of Reece and disgruntled that they weren't getting a fair chance at the queen's favor—or a fair shot at being the one to father my biological offspring.

What now?

Jason sat there looking at me like a hungry dog in the presence of a juicy steak, just waiting for his master's command to release his restraint and gobble it whole.

I closed my eyes, girding my strength.

Just get it over with. It's tradition. It's the way things are done. It doesn't mean anything. It's just your body—not your heart.

Pasting on a smile, I patted the bed covering beside me and ignored the fracturing feeling surrounding my heart.

"Jason... would you like to come sit over here?"

16

THE FIRST TIME

REECE

Though I was standing outside the door to Abbi's chambers, my ears—and every cell in my body—were attuned to what was going on *inside* it.

When Jason had arrived, responding to her summons, it had taken all my strength not to plant my fist in the center of his smiling face. He was all cleaned up, far better looking than I'd remembered him being.

The anticipation had been coming off him in waves. As for me, I was alternating between queasiness and sheer fury.

If Kannon hadn't also been posted outside the door, I would absolutely have told Jason the queen had changed her mind and sent him away. Instead, I'd nodded in acknowledgment and bitten my tongue as he entered the private chambers of *my* woman.

Of course she *wasn't* mine, could never *be* mine. Like just any other drone in the hive, I had no choice but to share Abbi with my Bloodbound brothers. Forever.

I really am going to go mad.

There had been some awkward small talk, then Jason

launched into some super-cheesy compliments, earning himself a few hundred extra laps during our next Bloodbound training exercises.

After that Abbi had invited him to sit with her on the bed, which felt like a thousand platinum-tipped arrows to my gut. The past few minutes had been quiet. Too quiet.

Which was bad. If they weren't talking, what *were* they doing?

My fists clenched, and my feet angled toward the door. Kannon's hand shot out to grab my shoulder before I could grasp the handle.

"Stay at your post," he advised. "I know it's hard, but it'll get easier. This is just the first time. You'll get used to it."

"Right. Like I got used to drinking from a blood bag instead of having a nice juicy ribeye for dinner."

In a swift, angry move, I turned back around to face the corridor, knocking the back of my skull repeatedly against the stone wall behind me to give myself something less painful to focus on.

The ringing in my head obscured a slight noise from Abbi's bedroom—it might have been a whisper. Or a kiss.

The next few minutes were a second-by-second battle for self-control, during which I imagined ever more creative and violent ways to murder Jason.

I was in the middle of a particularly pleasing vision involving pulling out his tongue and tying it in a bow around his neck when someone came rushing down the corridor toward us.

Kannon and I both sprang to full attention, crossing our swords in front of Abbi's door. Seconds later, we blew out simultaneous breaths of relief and lowered our weapons.

It was Heather, Abbi's close friend.

"Guys! Guys, I need to talk to Abbi—right now."

"What's going on?" Kannon demanded.

Heather gave us both a huge smile. "My boyfriend decrypted the flash drive. Y'all aren't going to *believe* what's on it." Glancing toward the door, she asked, "What's Abbi doing in there? She busy? Is this a bad time?"

I could have kissed Heather's puzzled face. "Not *at all*. In fact, your timing couldn't be better."

Nearly tearing the door off its hinges in my haste, I charged into Abbi's rooms but stopped before I got to the inner chamber that held her bed. I wasn't sure I wanted the image of... whatever was happening in there burned on my brain for eternity.

"My queen—there's something that needs your *immediate* attention," I called out.

To my great relief, Abbi appeared from around the corner, still dressed. Well, sort of dressed. She had on a silky black slip dress that molded to her curves like she'd been doused with black oil.

Was that *really* necessary?

Jason was so eager she could be wearing a beekeeping suit —complete with pith helmet and visor—and he'd have gladly jumped her.

"What's happening?" she asked.

Heather, who'd followed me in, rushed toward her and grabbed her forearms. "Abbi, we got into the flash drive. Cute nightgown by the way. Taking a nap?"

Abbi looked down at herself and blushed. "Sort of."

Just then, Jason came around the corner, shirtless and disgruntled looking. I fought the urge to bellow a triumphant laugh.

Sorry pal—party's over.

Heather's eyes popped wide, and she fell back a few steps. "Oh... sorry. I didn't mean to disturb your... whatever."

Abbi moved toward her, shaking her head rapidly.

"There's no 'whatever'—Jason was just showing me his tattoos."

Hmph. A growl escaped my throat.

"Where's the flash drive now?" Abbi asked.

"In the VHC office. Luis is there now. Abbi, you have to see it. No wonder Parker wanted it destroyed. I think it could change everything."

"You should get dressed." I'd meant to suggest it casually, but the *suggestion* came out sounding more like a command.

Abbi didn't seem to notice. If she did, she didn't take offense. She turned to Jason. "I'm sorry. I've got to go."

He gave her a tight-lipped smile then a nod before walking toward the door, pulling on his shirt as he went.

I managed to keep myself from doing a victory dance, but I couldn't prevent a satisfied smirk from invading my face. "I'll escort you to the VHC office, my queen," I said in a businesslike tone.

"Yes. Good," she said. "I want Kannon to come to. Jason?"

He turned back around, eyebrows raised in eager anticipation.

"Could you stay and guard my chamber door? We'll send another Bloodbound to stand watch with you," Abbi said.

The hope leaked from Jason's face again. His shoulders sagged. "Yes, my queen."

Kelly greeted us at the entrance to the cavern that served as the new VHC headquarters. "What took you guys so long? I'm *dying* to see what's on that flash. Luis won't even give me a peek."

The man emerged from a private office within the VHC cavern. "That's because I want my head to stay attached to my shoulders. My queen—I have the file open and ready for you to view it, if you'd like to step inside."

"Reece, you and Kannon come with me," Abbi said. "Heather, you too since you've already seen it."

At Kelly's disappointed pout, Abbi told her, "Let me get a look at it first—if I think you can see it without it endangering your life, I'll definitely let you. But it's likely Sadie died over whatever's on that flash drive. I don't want to put you at unnecessary risk."

When we were inside the office with the door closed behind us, Luis sat in an office chair in front of a laptop. "Ready?"

Abbi nodded, and he tapped the space bar, starting a video file. It only took a few minutes of viewing to understand why Parker had been willing to bomb an entire building full of humans and vampires to destroy it.

"Wow," Abbi breathed.

Turning away from the video, she looked at me. "I think this is the answer to our problems. We won't have to go to war with Parker. We're going to blackmail him."

17

SECRETS

Abbi

Of all the things I might have expected to see on the screen, this was not it.

The video showed President Graham Parker picking up streetwalkers—*vampire* streetwalkers. There was also some footage of Parker from inside a private room at a vampire massage parlor where there was a *lot* more than massages going on.

Pretty damning stuff.

There was no question it was him. His face was clearly identifiable. In the street video, you could even see Secret Service members in the car with him.

So the anti-vamp president was leading a double life. I didn't have to wonder what his followers would think if they knew—they'd hate it.

They certainly wouldn't vote for him again, and they might even contact their senators and representatives and demand he be impeached.

"This is exactly what we need," I said. "We can hold it over his head and use it to get him to re-open the dialogue between vampires and humans and honor the Crimson Accord."

"Are you *still* talking about a peaceful solution?" Kannon sounded incredulous. "I thought you said Sadie tried that already. He didn't meet with her—he had her killed."

"I have to agree with Kannon on this one. I think you should do what Imogen would have done," Reece said.

"Which is?"

"She'd disseminate this to every news media outlet in existence and put it on all the social media channels. Immediately. She'd bury him in the court of public opinion, turn his own supporters against him."

He grinned. "It'll be poetic justice."

Heather, who'd been quiet till now, spoke up. "If I may... working with the other VHC members here and monitoring what's already out there on social media and the various cable news outlets, I've learned something. Since the first day Parker began his presidential campaign, he's been training his followers to distrust the media—all of them who aren't in his pocket, that is. That's what dictators have done throughout history. They convince people the media can't be trusted then they have free reign to do whatever they want to do."

She shook her head sadly. "Even if you do release this footage to the public, his die-hard supporters are brainwashed. They'll see the evidence with their own eyes and *still* not believe it. He'll just say the video is doctored. He'll declare it all fake, and they'll believe him."

My shoulders slumped, and my head dropped forward. My lungs felt too tight.

"You're right. That's exactly what'll happen. I'm also worried that if he's cornered, he'll strike out in a panic. He'll enact *more* violence against vampires in this country. It might do more harm than good."

"So what are you going to do?" Reece asked.

"Parker has a false sense of security right now," I said. "I hate the direction things are going, but at least he's moving slowly. I'm going to wait until the Bloodbound numbers are back up where they need to be before I contact him and tell him what we've got on him."

Kannon let out a noise of frustration and threw his hands up in the air. "You're going to do nothing? You're still putting all your hopes on a cure, aren't you? Larkin said the research trials aren't going well."

"She also said setbacks are normal," I argued. "The breakthrough could happen any day. She's not giving up on the cure, and neither am I."

"For the record, I've *never* thought it was the answer," Kannon grumbled.

"We all know what you think," Reece said. "But Abbi is queen here, and she's spoken. We'll wait to contact Parker, and we'll continue to give Larkin and Nolan all the support they need as they work together toward a cure."

Kannon made another disgruntled noise but said nothing further.

A FEW NIGHTS LATER, Larkin sent word, asking me to come to the lab.

Had she done it? Had she finally managed to find a cure that would work for everyone and give all vampires the option of going back to their human state? I felt like I was floating rather than walking as I made my way through the caverns.

When I reached her workspace, my mood changed abruptly. Larkin didn't look triumphant. She looked terrified.

I dashed to her side. "What happened? Did you lose some more volunteers?"

She shook her head. "It's not that. There's something I need to tell you. Can I speak with you alone? I would have come to your chambers, but I didn't want your queensguard to overhear and tell the other Bloodbound."

Oh boy. This was going to be bad. Maybe she'd discovered it was impossible to cure vampirism after all?

"I would suggest going up to the surface and walking in the rose garden, but with that patrol of Parker's personal army so close by, Reece flips if I even get near the stairway to the surface these days."

I thought for a few seconds. "I know, let's go to the Rainbow Cave. We can talk there."

The cavern had always been one of my favorite spots at the Bastion. Featuring three beautiful flowing underground streams and a conveniently noisy thirty-foot-high waterfall, it would offer excellent sound camouflage for a private conversation.

"What about your guard detail?" Larkin asked, eying the two burly men who stood just outside the lab.

"I'll have them clear the Rainbow Cave then keep their distance. They won't be able to hear us."

Sure enough, when we sat on the large rocks that bordered the waterfall and stream, there was a noisy din of splashing water.

Still, when I asked her what was going on, Larkin answered in a low voice barely above a whisper.

"I'm pregnant, Abbi." Her eyes looked huge and dark and her face haunted.

"Oh."

For a minute that was all I could say. It was certainly not what I'd expected to hear.

Shortly after I'd arrived at the Bastion, Imogen had told

me that in the past some queens had become pregnant—and I knew from her journal that Sadie had. But she'd lost the baby.

Imogen had led me to believe other female vampires—the worker bees—couldn't even conceive. Since vampires all had liver failure, and the liver was what produced fetal blood during development, we were essentially an infertile species.

"How is that possible?" I asked Larkin. "You don't have queensblood."

She gave me a small smile. "See, that's the thing. I do. Or at least I did. I had *your* blood in my system—from when I got shot and you healed me. *Your* blood made me fertile, Abbi."

I blinked several times, processing the extraordinary words. Was it possible?

But then it sort of made sense. Imogen had given the Bloodbound her queensblood to make *them* fertile. Why wouldn't it do the same for female vampires?

Had Imogen *known* her blood would make the other women fertile and chosen to withhold it from them? It sounded like her, keeping a gift like that to herself.

"So did you take a pregnancy test? Do a blood test on yourself?" I asked. "How do you know?"

Larkin reached for my hand and slowly drew it to her abdomen, which now that her oversized shirt was pressed against it, I realized was quite distended.

"I *felt* the baby moving," she said. "Then I took a pregnancy test."

I kept my hand pressed to her belly, fascinated. "How far along are you?"

"I'm not exactly sure. I did an ultrasound on myself. The size and position of the fetus indicate it's about three quarters of the way through gestation, but I only missed my period a couple weeks ago."

"Wow. That's fast. Isn't it much too early for the baby to be that big already?"

"By human standards, yes," Larkin said. "But in vampire biology we learned about our connection to Africanized honeybees. And bees spend only three days in the egg then about twenty in the larval stage before they're mature. So who knows? It could be close. Which is why I finally got up the guts to tell you. Are you mad?"

"Mad? No—not at all." Throwing my arms around her shoulders, I pulled her close for a hug. "This is *great* news. Honestly. I'm thrilled for you."

Ending the hug and pulling back to see her face, I asked, "How do you feel? Are *you* happy?"

She nodded rapidly, smiling through tears. "I am. I really am. Scared to death, but happy."

"Have you told... "

I'd almost said "the father" but stopped myself. From what Imogen had taught me, vampire queens, like queen bees, needed a swarm of drones to conceive. It had to be the same in the case of Larkin's pregnancy as well.

She finished the question for me. "The father? No. He doesn't know yet." She laughed. "I didn't want to scare him."

I blinked in confusion. "You *know* who the father is?"

She made a funny face. "Of course. I haven't been with anyone else in years. Which brings up an interesting point... I wasn't with a swarm. It was just one guy. Which means Imogen lied to you—a swarm of drones isn't actually necessary for a queen to conceive."

"Oh wow, you're right."

Another of Imogen's self-serving lies. The implications of the truth hit me at the same time Larkin made her next observation.

"You could be pregnant right now, Abbi," she said

cheerfully. "We could both have babies, and our kids could grow up together."

My heart plummeted then sprang back up again, feeling like a living yo-yo in my chest.

"Now *I'm* scared."

"You shouldn't be. You'd be an amazing mom."

Whether that was true or not wasn't the issue. Yes, the thought of motherhood being a real possibility was wonderful, but I was suddenly aware this development wouldn't make the world safer for vampires—it would only make it *more* dangerous.

I didn't want to bring a child into that kind of world. I didn't want *Larkin's* child to be in danger either—or any other vampire baby.

There was no way I could stand by and do nothing or wait any longer. It was time to act. I had to reach out to President Parker and somehow convince him to stop persecuting vampires in this country before this brand-new generation was born.

"Will you give your blood to the other females?" Larkin asked. "I mean, it could make us a thriving race again. Before long we could catch up to the humans in number. Or do you still agree with Sadie's belief that the race was meant to go extinct?"

I didn't even have to think about my answer. "No—I don't think that anymore. How can I? I loved Sadie, but she was wrong. Your baby is proof positive the vampire race *is* supposed to exist and to go on. So yes, I'll share my blood with the other women. Seeing how happy you are just underlines for me that it's a gift—how could I keep it all for myself?"

Larkin beamed. "Sadie was right about one thing—you really are our last and greatest hope."

"Which terrifies me," I admitted. "But I can't run away from this any longer. It *was* my destiny to be queen all along."

I let out a small, desperate sounding laugh.

"What is it?" Larkin asked.

"Reece is going to be *so* smug about this."

"Yeah, you might get the 'I told you so' treatment. So, you're planning to tell him about the baby?"

"I think I have to. Even if I'm not pregnant, I'll need his help in dealing with Parker and his goons. As for telling other people... maybe it's good you haven't told the father yet, especially if you can't trust him not to brag about his *amazing* virility. This is great news, but it's also a powder keg. We should keep it under wraps for now. I don't want there to be any chance of President Parker getting wind of it before we're ready. I thought the sex tape would make him feel threatened—*this* will make him go ballistic. There *will* be a time and place to share the news. Will you trust me to choose it?"

Larkin rolled her eyes. "Of course I trust you. Why do you think you're the only person I've told?"

"Good. So does that mean you're also going to tell me who the baby's father is?"

Larkin cringed, but the pained expression was followed by a grin.

"I will... but you're not going to believe it."

18

SOMETHING BETTER TO THINK ABOUT

Reece

My belly boiled with nerves, and my heart felt like it weighed a thousand pounds as I walked to Abbi's chambers.

She'd summoned me, and I had an ominous feeling about the reason behind it.

Her first Bloodbound *liaison* with Jason a few days ago had been interrupted, but the need for the carnal visits hadn't changed. The threat against our race from hostile humans was still growing, and our defensive forces were still dwindling.

She was going to ask me to select another soldier—or tell me she'd chosen someone from among the ranks.

I knew it was necessary. What I didn't know was how I was going to stand it. I could never join the defectors and leave the Bastion—leave *her*—but I honestly wasn't sure I could survive for eternity, standing by while she took a succession of lovers.

I'd go insane and have to be put down like a rogue.

Why had I convinced her to take on the role and duties of queen? Survival of the species was a noble goal—in theory.

In reality, it was breaking my heart one jagged piece at a time.

Nodding to the guards outside her door, I went in, that battered heart pounding in my ears like the bass of my Charger's sound system.

You can do this. One night at a time. Whatever she says, keep your cool.

I found Abbi sitting at the end of her bed. She looked gorgeous, as always. Tonight she wore a skirt with a black bandeau top that exposed her shoulders as well as her waist and stomach, which made it even more painful to picture her with one of my so-called *brothers*.

No doubt whichever lucky fellow found himself here alone with her later tonight would be gaping at every luscious inch of exposed skin. An involuntary growl rolled through my chest.

Calm. Down.

Don't think about it.

"My queen," I said in a tone of barely controlled fury. "You summoned me?"

Abbi actually laughed. "Did someone pee in your blood bag or something?"

Working to modulate my voice, I said, "I'm sorry. I was just thinking of something that made me angry."

"Well, let me give you something better to think about then."

For a moment I got my hopes up. Had she summoned me for *that* reason? But then she stood and walked away from the bed.

"I have some news..."

Oh God, here it was. She was going to tell me about the next Bloodbound who'd be called to her quarters for his turn.

"I'm not sure how to lead into this gently, so I'm just going to say it... Larkin is pregnant."

I think my eyes literally bulged from my head. "What?"

Of all the things I'd been expecting Abbi to say, that wasn't even in the team picture.

"How? I mean, I *know* how babies are made, but I thought it was impossible for vampires."

She shook her head. "Nope, it's very possible. She may be only a week or two from delivering."

Shaking my head, I mumbled, "Kannon, you dog."

"Wait... you knew?"

"I suspected. He acted too strangely when I said her name. Plus I know what a guy looks like when he's in love—I see it every time I look in the mirror. So... what does this mean? Is Larkin Sadie's daughter or something?"

"No, but that's a really good guess. Remember when I gave her my blood after she was shot? She had it in her system, and that made her fertile."

"But... wouldn't she have to be with like, lots of guys?" I asked.

"She says Kannon was the only one."

I thought for a minute. "Imogen must have made up the part about needing a swarm so she could justify keeping all the most eligible males for herself in what amounted to a harem."

"Exactly. And while she shared her blood with them in an attempt to make them fertile so she could get pregnant, she never shared it with any of the females."

"I don't think a more selfish woman ever lived. I'm glad the cure killed her. Speaking of that, has Larkin made any more progress?"

"Not really, but it doesn't matter anymore," Abbie said. "I'm going to tell her to stop working on it. I don't know why I couldn't see it earlier vampires don't need to be fixed or changed. What we need is a blood substitute, so we don't deplete the human race. It's more important now than ever... because I think there's going to be a vampire baby boom."

Very slowly, a smile overtook my lips. I let out a bark of laughter and then a whoop, grabbing Abbi's shoulders.

"I knew it. I knew it was meant to be. You've saved us."

She blushed. "Well not quite yet. I can help vampires procreate, but I've still got to figure out a way to keep them safe from the humans who hate them. It can't wait any longer —I *have* to talk to Parker. He's not going to change—and we can't just sit here and wait for him to find us and slaughter our people or send them all to prison camps."

My elation dimmed. "He won't like this development—at all. He and the other haters are going to see it as a dire threat to the human race. It might even speed up his attempt to eradicate us and win him even more support from the humans who are scared of us or just plain don't like us."

"I agree, which is why I'm not going to tell him about Larkin's baby," Abbie said. "But I am going to try one more time to reason with him. He *knows* the sex tapes are real— maybe the guilt alone will be enough to get him to listen to reason. It's a risk, but we have to know once and for all if there can be peace with him or if it's going to come to war."

I frowned. "I'm afraid I already know which one of the two it'll be."

"Me too, which is why I'm hoping my best Bloodbound soldier will accompany me when I meet with him."

19

NO TIME TO CRY

Abbi

Unfortunately the president had no intention of meeting with me, which became clear when we spoke by phone.

Reece and I drove to Washington D.C. two hours away to make the call. I certainly didn't want to make it from the Bastion or anywhere near it, in case the call was traced.

To prevent the cell signal from being triangulated, Reece kept the car in motion while I made the call on a burner phone. We could get out of the city quickly enough when it was done.

If the call *was* traced to a location right there in D.C., we figured the Secret Service and other authorities would be freaked out enough that they'd thoroughly scrub the city before spreading out and searching the surrounding cities and states.

Knowing better than to identify myself as queen of the vampires, I told the White House operator I was the head of the VHC—which was probably the only reason Parker took the call.

"Sadie?" His voice sounded incredulous. "I'd heard you

met with an unfortunate accident—I guess I was misinformed."

"Hello Mr. President. This is Abigail Byler. I'm the *new* head of the Vampire-Human Coalition of America."

Now he sounded amused. And much more relaxed.

"Miss Byler, I'm not sure how you can be the new leader of the Vampire-Human Coalition since there's no longer any such organization."

Channeling my inner Sadie, I kept my tone low and even. "I assure you there is, sir, and we are just as committed as ever to preserving and increasing peace and cooperation between the races. Which is why I'd like to schedule a meeting with you to discuss our grievances and talk about how we can work together to better uphold the tenets of the Crimson Accord."

The man had the gall to chuckle. "You may have a handful of delusional do-gooders with you, but after that *unfortunate* incident in Los Angeles, my sources tell me the majority of your members are either dead or scattered to the wind and hiding. You simply don't have the numbers, honey—which means there's just no reason for me to waste my valuable time taking a meeting with you."

Ugh. He was so smug, so sure he'd won.

"I can think of a few reasons. One—it's the right thing to do. If that doesn't interest you, then maybe you'd be interested in a flash drive that's come into my possession. It contains some rather shocking footage of vampire prostitutes and a prominent politician who's built his entire platform on stoking human hatred of vampires."

All traces of humor left Parker's voice. "There is no such footage. Even if there was, it wouldn't matter—I'm untouchable. My supporters are so loyal I'm practically a god to them. They're more invested in me than the country itself.

I'm the greatest president in American history, and *you*—you are no one but a nasty little vamp."

I honestly thought he was going to hang up on me following his rant, but after a pause, he asked, "Where'd you say that new headquarters is located?"

"I didn't. I urge you to reconsider your position on this, Mr. President. We want peace between the species, but not at any cost. I'm not going to stand by forever while my people are mistreated and discriminated against."

His tone shifted from boredom to malice. "Are you threatening me, young lady? The last uppity female vamp who threatened me found herself on the *crispy* side of the bed."

I sucked in a sharp breath, unable to speak for a moment. He'd just basically confessed to Sadie's murder.

There was no working with this man. He was pure evil. He was never going to come to any sort of terms with us.

Reece and Kannon had been right all along—it was going to come to war.

"You did it, didn't you?" I said. "You killed one of the kindest souls to ever walk this earth. You're not going to get away with it."

"And you," he said with a sneer I could literally hear over the phone, "have just made a threat against the life of a sitting president. By the way, while we've been speaking, I had my people look you up. You're a wanted criminal, Miss Byler. You dropped off the radar there for a while, but you better believe you're smack dab in the center of it now with a big old bullseye on your back."

I ended the call and threw the burner phone out the car window. Then Reece backed up the car and rolled it forward, crushing the phone under its front tire before getting on the highway.

Just in case, we switched vehicles outside the city before driving home to the Bastion.

When we were on the highway, Reece looked over at me. "That didn't sound good."

"No. Not at all. He's definitely *not* open to peace talks. And now that I've provoked him and identified myself, he's not going to rest until he finds me and the new VHC. When we get home, I want you to arrange a gathering of the Bastion's full population."

"Of course. What are you going to tell them? That we're going to war with the humans? You know I'll back you whatever you decide, and I'll defend you to the death, but I don't have to tell you that our troop numbers are far too low. It's going to be a mismatch of epic proportions."

"Trust me," I said. "I have a plan."

BEFORE FACING the Bastion's citizens and making perhaps the most important speech of my life, I took a few minutes to gather my thoughts then opened Sadie's journal for one last bit of inspiration.

The entries skipped around through the years. While it was fascinating to read about her alliance with President John F. Kennedy that led to the signing of the Crimson Accord, I turned to the final entry in her journal. It was dated during the time Kelly, Heather, and I worked at the VHC.

I HAVEN'T ENTIRELY GIVEN **up on peace between vampires and humans, but it seems the struggle is never-ending. I am weary of the fight.**

Sometimes I wonder if my sister was right all along. Perhaps I should have focused more on the power that

comes with vampirism and been proud of who we are instead of apologizing and trying to acclimate to the rigid standards of human society.

The fact is, we are different, and perhaps those differences should be celebrated instead of sanitized.

I am coming to the point where I must admit my peace-at-all-costs approach has been too costly. I'm afraid I have failed the vampire race.

But I do still have hope. I believe I have found the one who is going to save all our people. Surprisingly, she is Imogen's child, but she is not like my sister. Not like me, either.

Abigail is unique, and I truly believe she will change the world with her own unique approach.

CLOSING THE BOOK, I held it to my chest and breathed in and out slowly as I fought tears. Swiping at my face, I blinked them away. This was no time to cry.

It was time to address my people, to learn whether Sadie's faith in me was justified and if Imogen had chosen well when she decided to claim me as her heir.

Rising from the bed, I strode toward the door and then down the corridor that led to the Grand Dome.

Only one way to find out.

2 0

THE POWER OF OUR PEOPLE

REECE

The last time the Grand Dome had been this full was Abbi's first address to the citizens of the Bastion. I desperately hoped tonight's speech would go better, but I feared it would not.

The news she'd delivered before was at least hopeful—that there might be a cure and that they were all going to be okay.

Now she couldn't say either of those things. The cure had turned out to be a bust, and Parker was more motivated than ever to ferret out our stronghold.

Eventually he'd succeed.

No doubt the U.S. military would be joining his private army in the search. They knew we had to shelter from the sunlight during the day and had already searched some of the region's other caverns.

It wouldn't be long before they found this one.

Though I would stand by Abbi no matter what she did or said to the people tonight, I was afraid she'd waited too late to give the people the war they wanted. Our own military forces had waned to the point we stood no chance.

In contrast, the population of civilians in the Bastion had grown exponentially. Looking out over the sea of faces in the Grand Dome tonight, I was nearly overwhelmed by the size of the crowd.

So many. So many lives at risk.

There was a dull roar of conversation as the gathered vampires speculated on why their new queen had called them together. It quieted when she entered the auditorium chamber.

Unlike the first time Abbi had stood before her people, there was no shaking. Her hands and her voice were completely calm.

She stood for a moment, surveying the assembly. Then she spoke, loud and clear.

"My friends… I have promised you that I would lead you to the best of my ability and do so with honesty. The truth tonight is that I come before you with bad news. I have spoken with President Parker. His hatred for our kind has only grown, and he has been emboldened by the destruction of the VHC headquarters and by the assassination of its leader, Imogen's sister Sadie, who was my dear friend. In fact, Parker claimed responsibility for both and has no remorse."

Abbi took a long pause, her expression growing sad. "Sadie believed in peace, and so do I… to a point. I want us to have peace, but if the vampire people are going to survive and thrive, we must also have power."

There was an explosion of noise. The gathered vampires clapped and chanted, some yelling for war, some for assassination of the hateful president.

Abbi held up a hand, quieting the room again. "I used to think a cure for vampirism was the answer, that it would be so much easier if we could go back to being human, to being 'acceptable' in the eyes of humans, but I've changed my mind about that as well. Even if someone does create a reliable cure someday, I will not be taking it. Because I no longer believe we need one. We don't need to be cured—we are *not* a disease. We are *people*. Yes, we're different from the humans, but that doesn't make us 'wrong.' We were meant to be in this world, and we deserve to be treated with as much respect and dignity as all other people."

The crowd's clamor, which had sounded aggressive and bloodthirsty before, was now exuberant.

"Now is a time of grave danger," Abbi continued. "President Parker is coming for us. Right now his personal army is searching out our sanctuary. If they find us, I will tell you honestly, we don't have enough Bloodbound soldiers to hold them off."

The throng's enthusiastic cheers hushed.

Abbi remained undeterred and serene. "You've probably noticed their numbers dwindling, and I'll tell you why it's happened. Imogen used to give the soldiers her blood to keep them loyal—to brainwash them. I chose not to do that. I didn't want to coerce loyalty from anyone. I wanted to earn it. I don't want to enslave our people but to *free* them."

Walking to the other side of the platform, Abbi wore a sad smile.

"At the beginning of my reign, I was advised that compelling the Bloodbound with queensblood and mating with all the drones was the way of the vampire species, the way it's 'always been done.'"

Now her smile grew wide and triumphant. "Well, just because something's *always* been a certain way doesn't mean it's the only way or even the best way. The world is always changing, and I believe we should change with it. I told you we *must* have power—but I don't see power as one person lording it over the rest. Rather, I see it as a community working together and combining individual strengths to create a force more powerful than one person could ever be."

Abbi's voice increased in volume and passion as she went on. "We need more soldiers—but I *will not* compel any of you with my queensblood. Instead I am asking you to volunteer to serve and protect of your own free will. I encourage anyone—male or female—who desires to protect the vulnerable members of our community to come forward and begin Bloodbound training."

Whether from shock at Abbi's unprecedented invitation or reluctance regarding the well-known celibacy requirement, there wasn't an immediate rush to volunteer.

"Oh, I should mention..." Abbi said with a sneaky smile, "... I'm putting an end to the rule that Bloodbound take no mate aside from the queen. In fact, all current and future Bloodbound soldiers are encouraged to take a permanent mate of their own."

Now there were cheers and an outpouring of bodies into the center aisle. Abbi motioned for me to come and stand beside her. When I did, she shocked me by grasping my hand, holding onto it as we stood side by side in front of the Bastion's entire population.

"How could I deny my faithful soldiers that right when I myself have chosen a permanent mate, and he has chosen me," she announced.

She raised her arm, taking mine with it until our clasped hands were high above our heads for all to see.

"One more thing," Abbi said. "Not only will all of you be able to take a mate... many of you will become parents."

There was a collective gasp followed by a hush so that Abbi's next words could be clearly heard.

"Though I will not use my blood to control you, I *will* be

sharing it with anyone who wants it. You see, queensblood serves another purpose. Larkin..."

Abbi turned toward the back of the platform where Larkin was just emerging from the queen's private entrance.

It had been a few weeks since I'd seen Abbi's friend, and even though I knew about the pregnancy, the vast changes in Larkin's body took me by surprise.

She appeared ready to give birth at any moment.

When she came into public view, there was a swell of sound, astonished gasps, admiring oohs and ahhhs. Larkin came to a stop beside Abbi who used her free hand to pull her friend in for a side-hug.

"It turns out queensblood makes vampire males *and* females fertile. Anyone who wants to become a parent will have the opportunity."

A full-on celebration broke out in the Grand Dome.

There was literal dancing and so much jubilant noise I didn't hear Chase or see him coming until he'd reached the front of the platform where Abbi and Larkin stood hugging.

"For King Parker! Stake the traitors—down with the false queen!"

The Bloodbound solider we'd banished let out a war cry and drew his sword as he jumped onto the platform, rearing back to swing the weapon at Abbi's throat.

Before I had time to even think about it, my right hand drew the dagger from my belt, and I hurled it at the would-be assassin.

The platinum-tipped blade struck him in the side of the neck, causing him to fall.

Unfortunately the momentum he'd already accrued carried him forward, propelling him directly into Larkin and knocking her down.

Abbie screamed, "Larkin!"

Kannon was instantly in motion, leaping onto the

platform and dragging the dead attacker's body off of her. He fell to his knees beside the hugely pregnant vampire.

"Larkin! Larkin baby, you okay?"

Kannon cradled her head, propping up the top half of her body and searching her face. His displayed utter terror.

Larkin reached up and stroked his jaw with one hand. "Yes. I think he just knocked the wind out of me—oh wow!"

Her eyelids flared, and her lips contracted to form a small "o."

"What is it?" Kannon demanded. "Something hurt? Did he break a rib?"

She smiled, then winced. "No, but your son might if he gets any bigger. Fortunately I think he's ready to come out."

Kannon's face went white as pure calcite. "Labor pains?"

Larkin nodded and winced again. "Pretty sure that's what they are. Either that or I ate a potful of beans I forgot about."

Dr. Coppa appeared, having made his way through the crowd toward the platform. "Let's get her to the clinic. The labor and delivery room has been set up and ready since I first learned about her condition."

Kannon nodded then scooped Larkin up in one easy move, carrying her in a cradle hold as he followed the doctor.

"We'll be right there," Abbi called after them.

We exchanged a glance that encompassed all the fear—and relief—we were both feeling.

"You're okay?" I asked.

"I'm fine," she assured me. "I guess when we banished him, he joined up with Parker. How did he get back in here?"

Glancing down at the dead vampire I nodded, frowning. "I'm not sure. But we have to find out—fast. And we've got to assume the president's troops know where we are now."

She nodded gravely. "I'm going to say a few more words and then we can both go to the clinic to check on Larkin."

Turning back to the masses of shell-shocked vampires, Abbi once again exuded confidence and determination.

"Obviously President Parker hasn't stopped and *won't* stop until we convince him it's in his best interests. Apparently, the only way to do that is fight back. Who's ready to show him the power of our people?"

A roar of approval ricocheted around the Dome.

Abbi raised one arm over her head, beaming. "Who's ready to join the Bloodbound and defend the vampire race?"

More cheers and battle cries.

"Who's ready to go. To. War?"

A deafening roar punctuated by chants of "Queen Abigail" reverberated through the cavern and made my heart swell with pride.

For the first time in a long time... it was joined by a sense of hope.

NEWEST SOLDIER

Abbi

Attending a birth was a new thing for me.

Growing up Amish, I had many younger siblings and had been in the house during all their births, but only my father and a midwife had been in the room with Maam during the actual labor and delivery.

In our culture, pregnancy and childbirth were considered private things and were somewhat of a mystery to girls until it was their turn to participate as expectant mothers themselves.

Thankfully the Bastion had a resident who'd been a midwife in her human life. She'd presented herself at the medical clinic following the assembly in the Grand Dome, offering her services.

Several nurses and doctors worked at the clinic, but none had specialized in obstetrics in their former lives, so her offer was accepted with gratitude.

Reece and I sat in the waiting room, and Kannon came out every couple of hours to give us updates.

"Did they say the baby is full term?" I asked, concerned

that Larkin's estimated gestation timeline put her at only a few weeks along.

It might have been fine—none of us had any idea what a "normal" vampire pregnancy looked like—but I was worried the baby might be premature.

He nodded. "They just did an ultrasound, and they're estimating his weight at about eight pounds, so yeah, he's fully cooked. Anyway, based on the size of Larkin's belly, I guessed she had to be getting near the end."

"I hope you didn't say that to her," I scolded.

Kannon laughed. "Do I look crazy to you? No, I just kept telling her how beautiful she was. Anyway, I better get back in there if I want to preserve my ability to father any *future* children. I'll keep you posted."

Finally, about four hours later, one of the nurses stepped into the waiting room. She was smiling widely.

"Larkin's asking for you. Ready to come meet the little miracle man?"

Reece and I leapt from our chairs and followed her into the delivery room. Larkin was in the bed, looking exhausted but happy. Kannon stood beside her, cradling his tiny, swaddled son in his arms.

"How are you doing?" I asked my friend.

"Great. I mean, not *all* of it was great." Larkin laughed. "But that's how you get a baby, right? And he's worth it."

"He sure is. You did awesome, babe." Kannon shifted his gaze from her to smile down into the baby's face. "Daniel, say hello to your queen."

Then glancing up at me, he said, "Meet your newest soldier."

Kannon had meant it as a gesture of respect, a nice moment, but the comment stung me like a hard slap across the face.

Seeing him holding his new baby and smiling sweetly

over at Larkin with tears in his eyes, I was rocked by a powerful realization.

I didn't want little Daniel growing up with the prospect of war hanging over his perfect, innocent head.

People *died* in war, and a war between humans and vampires was bound to be very deadly indeed.

I didn't want *any* of the Bloodbound—not Kannon and certainly not Reece—to die in battle.

There had to be a better way.

Taking in the beautiful scene of Kannon, Larkin, and their child sharing their first few minutes of life together as a family, I was struck with an idea. Maybe there was a way to have both peace *and* power.

"Want to hold him?" Kannon asked.

I nodded and accepted the tiny bundle, marveling over the lightness of the baby, the fragility and utter perfection. Though he'd been sleeping, the newborn opened his lids and stared up at me with hazy, lilac-colored eyes. Mine filled with tears.

"Hello Daniel," I said. "Welcome to the world. You don't know it yet, but we're going to make it a better place —together."

To the new parents, I said, "Congratulations. He's perfect."

Placing the baby into Larkin's waiting arms, I turned to Reece and tilted my head toward the door. "We should give them some privacy. Larkin, let me know if there's anything you need while you recover. Kannon, feel free to take a few weeks leave from the Bloodbound."

He gave me a quizzical glance. "But the war..."

"We'll talk about that later. Don't worry. I promise I won't ride into battle without you."

Silently I added an addendum.

And I think I've come up with a way to avoid battle altogether.

2 2

———

THE REAL REASON

Reece

Abbi had been amazing throughout the assembly. Actually, it had turned into more of a pep rally thanks to her charisma and empowering leadership.

And when she'd publicly claimed me as her permanent mate, I literally couldn't have been happier. It took all the self-discipline I possessed not to grab her and kiss her right there in front of the masses.

If we could have stayed here in the Bastion forever together, with Abbi leading her devoted followers in peace and safety, everything would have been perfect.

But we couldn't. And things were far from perfect.

Graham Parker's special forces were breathing down our necks. Peace and safety were teetering on a razor-thin wire that could snap any day. As her top advisor—and her mate—I had to make sure Abbi understood our precarious position.

The med clinic's waiting room hadn't been the place to discuss it, but once we were alone in her chambers, I let the pent-up tension out.

"We need to talk about our defensive strategy."

She gave me an untroubled smile and sat on the edge of her bed. "Okay."

I couldn't sit. Adrenaline had me pacing as I explained.

"Thanks to your incredible recruitment effort tonight, our numbers are looking a lot better, but the new Bloodbound volunteers are raw and untrained. No matter how many there are or how enthusiastic they are, it'll take weeks to get them up to speed—longer, maybe, since most of them have no military or law enforcement background and some won't be in fighting condition."

"I understand."

Why didn't Abbi look more concerned?

Scooting back on the bed, she relaxed against the large collection of pillows and stroked the bed covering, smoothing out the wrinkles she'd just created.

"They won't need to be in fighting condition. I have a new plan."

"You do?"

She nodded. "First, I'm going to make a few phone calls. Sadie told me there are vampire queens in pretty much every country, and I think it's high time we all had a chat. Then I'm going to reach out to President Parker again and request a meeting—and this time, I won't take no for an answer."

Now I was even more worried. "He threatened your life. He hinted he'd wipe you out just like he did Sadie."

"He won't hurt me. I'm going to convince him that he needs me alive."

"How will you do *that*?" I asked, baffled. "The blackmail attempt didn't work. He wasn't threatened by the sex tape. Even if he does agree to a meeting, I don't know what good it'll do—like you said, his mind's not going to change. He hates us, and he always will. He won't rest until vampires are wiped from the face of the earth."

Abbi smiled, her eyes glinting with confidence. "That's

what I'm counting on. I'm going to tell him there's a way to *do* that, and that I'll ensure our willing *participation* in the effort. I'm going to tell him there's a cure and that we need his help to disseminate it to vampires nationwide."

My jaw slackened. "The cure doesn't even work."

"The president doesn't know that—and he won't find out. Not until it's too late and my *real* reason for meeting with him personally is revealed."

***

PARKER TOOK THE BAIT—HUNGRILY.

A week after Kannon and Larkin's baby was born, Abbi and I were walking through the White House toward the West Wing. Our Bloodbound bodyguards had been forced to wait outside, but Abbi said she wasn't afraid for our safety.

"It's worth the risk," she'd said. "Two lives instead of potentially millions lost, right?"

"Right." I'd nodded, though in my mind her life was worth millions of others.

Together we stepped into the Oval Office, taking seats in the chairs our escorts offered. The president and his vice president, a man who didn't seem as hateful but also didn't publicly contradict Parker and his policies, were already there, sitting on a low couch opposite us.

Secret service agents stood in every corner of the room, hands on their anti-vamp weapons, ready to fire should things take a bad turn.

"Well..." the president began, "I have to say, you've got courage showing up here this evening. I was surprised but very pleased when you reached out to me for help, Miss Byler. We can't get rid of this vampire infection fast enough. We'll dedicate all the resources necessary to help—the National Guard to distribute it, I can enable the Defense

Production Act to manufacture more, whatever it takes to restore this country to the great human nation it once was."

Abbi gave him a placid smile. "I think it still *is* a great nation—or at least it can be if we keep moving forward. And I do need your help... but not with distributing a cure. There isn't one, by the way."

I could almost see the question marks floating above Parker's head. "What are you talking about?"

He looked from her to me to his vice president then back to her again. "That's what we're here for, isn't it?"

"Actually," Abbi said, "I came here to sign a *new* version of the Crimson Accord."

She nodded toward me, and I pulled the amended document from my bag, handing it to Parker.

Since I'd worked on it with a team of vampire lawyers at the Bastion, I knew it called for better enforcement of the original Accord's protections for vampires, plus the immediate release of all detainees at the so-called Safety Centers, the return of all vampire property illegally confiscated by the federal government, and the restoration of jobs to all the vampires fired without just cause.

Looking perplexed, Parker thumbed through the pages, stopping to read a paragraph or two before chuckling.

"Why exactly would I sign this?"

He tossed the stack of papers onto the low table in front of him. "I didn't like the first one. I like this version even less."

Abbi leaned in, offering him a pen. "You'll sign it because it's the best thing for all Americans, humans and vampires alike. You'll also agree to stop agitating the anti-vamp sentiment in the country and to clamp down on violence and discrimination against vampires. In fact, you'll be giving a national televised address on the importance of peace between the species and respect for one another."

She held up a finger and smiled. "Oh, and one more thing... you won't be running for re-election."

She was so calm—a total badass. I couldn't have been prouder.

Parker, on the other hand, was losing his cool.

"You are a piece of work, little lady. I won't do *any* of this nonsense, and I *will* be running for re-election—and winning. As a matter of fact, I'm considering doing away with the two-term limit and *staying* in office as long as I damn well please. The people of this country are behind me. I have a public mandate to restore this country to its pre-Accord greatness, and I intend to do that. Vague threats from some little vamp tart aren't going to stop me."

Muscles tensed all over my body, and even my veins strained against my skin. It would be *so* easy to tear this guy's limbs off and beat him with them.

Abbi raised her hand slightly in a gesture I knew was meant to calm me. Closing my eyes, and gritting my teeth, I willed myself to relax back into my chair.

"Do you feel I'm being vague? Well let me clear up any ambiguity for you," Abbi said. "The majority of people in this country are *not* behind you. The new VHC has been doing some grassroots outreach and voter polling. Most Americans want vampires and humans to live in peace and think vampires deserve equal rights."

"The VHC is nothing. I wiped it out before, and I can do it again. *That's* how you deal with an infestation," Parker said emphatically.

"I know a little something about getting rid of vermin myself," Abbi said, remaining completely cool and in control. "I grew up on a farm, and we had problems with mice from time to time. There were just so *many* of them. You know what did the trick? Getting a few cats. Did you know the average free-roaming cat kills about ninety small animals a year? They're the natural predator of mice and birds... much like vampires are the natural predators of humans."

"Are you trying to threaten me?"

"No, I'm simply informing you of the facts. You said to me before that we didn't have the numbers. You're wrong. There are far more vampires than you realize. And your followers are actually a small minority of the overall American population—they're just very loud about their bigotry and hatred, especially when you lie to them and whip them into a frenzy."

Parker pointed at her, spittle forming at the corners of his mouth as he ranted.

"There's enough of them to win an election—especially when the other party splits the vote between candidates. That's all that matters. My people *go to the polls* on election day, and they're loyal to me and *only* me."

"Would they be, do you think, if they actually knew the *real* you?" Abbi asked.

Parker blanched but made a speedy comeback. "If you think you're going to scare me with that video you have of me fooling around with vamp whores, you can forget it. It doesn't matter *what* you have on me. My followers won't believe it, even if they see it with their own eyes. They care more about what I say than any sort of proof you or anyone else might be able to dig up."

His face split into a smile so big and so evil he resembled a jack-o-lantern. "I can do anything I want to—literally anything—and my followers will still believe whatever I say and love me and re-elect me."

He chuckled and puffed out his chest. "I could even kill you right here and now—do it in a live broadcast if I wanted to. I could stake you out there in the middle of Pennsylvania Avenue in front of a crowd of witnesses and still get away with it."

Okay, that's it.

I cocked my head from side to side and rolled my shoulders, ready to take the man down. The vice president too—and all the Secret Service members. No one was going to stake Abbi. Not while I lived.

She didn't appear to be shaken at all, and her voice stayed tranquil.

"You *could* kill me, that's true. But there will always be another me. You will *never* eradicate the vampire race. Just as with the barn cats, biology is on our side."

"Hardly." Parker smirked. "That Crimson Accord you love so much stipulates vampires can't lawfully turn humans, so if you keep to the law, there aren't going to be any more of you made. There's only one way that's going to turn out for the vampires. Your numbers are going to go *down*—and keep going down. Eventually, you're going to die out and disappear."

Abbi smiled. "Are we?" Nodding toward the window, she said, "Go take a look."

The Secret Service guys moved first, rushing to the three large, south-facing windows to look down on the south lawn of the White House.

"Sir, you need to see this," one of them said.

President Parker and the vice president got up and went to the windows. Though we already knew what was out there, I did the same, just for fun.

It was an incredible sight to behold.

The vast stretch of green known as the South Lawn was the location of the annual White House egg-rolling contest and the landing area for the president's helicopter, Marine One.

Now it was covered with people—most of them vampires, but some humans too.

Floodlights illuminated a shoulder-to-shoulder swarm

stretching all the way to South Executive Drive and across it, filling the Ellipse, a fifty-two-acre circular public park south of the White House.

"Where the hell did they all come from? *How* did they all get here?" Parker demanded. "I looked out the window just before the meeting, and there wasn't a soul out there aside from our security staff."

One member of his protection detail shrugged apologetically. "They're vampires, sir. They can pretty much go anywhere they want. And they're fast. If they decide to occupy an area, there's really nothing we can do to prevent it."

"You see, Mr. President," Abbi said. "The Crimson Accord, including its prohibition on large gatherings by vampires, has only worked because we've *chosen* to abide by it. If you continue to violate its tenets, my people are going to decide there's no point in them obeying it any longer."

Parker whirled to face her. "They'll see the point when my soldiers start blowing them away."

Abbi didn't even flinch. "Yes, you have anti-vamp weapons, but as with anything, if enough people get together and decide to do something, there's no stopping them. Wave after wave will come at you until your defenses are overwhelmed. What you see is only a *fraction* of the vampires who are ready, willing, and able to stand up for our rights and fight if necessary. As their queen..."

She raised a single eyebrow and waited a beat to let that phrase sink in before going on. "... I am uniting vampire-kind nationwide *and* have made contact with vampire queens in other countries as well. And we won't be alone. The VHC's offices have been overwhelmed by human allies who want to help."

Her deliberate pause was drawn out and dramatic. "I

imagine those numbers will only increase once they realize there are innocent *newborn* lives at stake as well."

She pointed to the window, and Parker turned to look outside again.

At the front of the crowd, surrounded by a protective ring of Bloodbound guards but still visible from our vantage point, stood Larkin and Kannon and their infant son.

Kannon raised one of Daniel's tiny hands and moved it in a wave.

"Is that a... is that a *baby?*" the stunned president asked.

"That's right. And that happy couple is only the first," Abbi said. "There are already scores of other vampire couples who've conceived. Quite a few of them will be making appearances tonight on the national news and late-night talk shows to show off their sonograms and baby bumps. They've already taped their interviews, but these two—and their son —will be appearing together on the morning shows tomorrow. *All* of them."

"We're through running and hiding," she continued. "Whether or not there's ever a viable cure, a lot of vampires can't go back, and many have no interest in changing. Which is why the world is going to have to change to accept us."

Graham Parker stood and stared, his jaw slack as Abbi continued.

"*That,* sir, will be your presidential legacy. Without meaning to, you've brought unity to our respective species. Congratulations, Mr. President."

23

POWER AND PEACE

Three months later

Reece and I sat on our bed, surrounded by colorful wrapping paper and ribbons—and stacks of unopened gift boxes and bags.

Since I'd gone public with my role as queen—and my pregnancy—world leaders and civilian well-wishers alike had been showering Reece and me with baby gifts. New ones arrived each day.

So many had piled up in our private chambers it was hard to find room to move. I'd actually tripped over an enormous stuffed bumble bee last night while walking to get Sadie out of her crib to feed her.

Like many of the expanding families here in the Bastion, we were feeling the need for more elbow room.

Thankfully many of them had been able to go back to their homes, their old jobs, and communities.

Many others—perhaps *too* many—had elected to stay in this isolated sanctuary. I was beginning to wonder if my role as their leader was due for a shift—from "queen bee" to "mama bird."

But how to go about pushing them from the nest? And when?

Opening a box, Reece laughed. "Another diaper disposal system. Thank God we don't need it."

One benefit of vampire babies—in addition to the fact most of them quickly moved past the waking every two hours stage—was the fact that their bodies used mother's milk the same way our adult bodies used blood. It simply absorbed into their systems with no waste. Having washed and line-dried my fair share of cloth diapers as an Amish big sister, I would be eternally grateful.

"Put it in the donation pile with the others," I said. "There are plenty of human parents who will *love* it, I'm sure."

Dragging a bag onto my lap, I pulled out the tissue paper and reached inside. When I drew out the gift, Reece and I both stared at it.

It was an autographed picture of President Parker, in an engraved silver frame. The personalized signature read, "For baby Sadie, from your friend, President Graham Parker."

"How thoughtful." I wrinkled my nose. "I guess we can't regift this one."

Reece laughed. "Who would want it?"

"Do you think he likes us now? Or maybe it has something to do with that recording you got of him admitting the video of him with prostitutes was real and bragging that he could kill me and literally get away with murder," I quipped.

Reece shrugged, not looking the least bit guilt-ridden. "He was so busy threatening you he didn't notice what I was doing."

I leaned against my handsome mate, wrapping my arms around his shoulders. "That was stupid of him. Everyone knows you shouldn't trust a rogue vampire."

"I'll show you a rogue." Reece laughed again and kissed

me passionately, pushing my shoulders gently back to the pillows.

"Wait—we don't have time." I struggled upright again. "We have to go present Sadie to her people."

"What's another few hours? They can wait." Reece kissed my neck again.

With regret, I wriggled from his hold and got out of bed. "They've played the pipe organ. People are gathering in the Grand Dome already. Besides, Sadie will wake up any second."

Directing a fond look at the crib, Reece smiled at his daughter, who was indeed beginning to stir and kick her tiny feet in the air.

"Well, now that's different. Daddy's girl doesn't wait for anyone." He rolled out of bed and went to the crib, scooping Sadie up and nuzzling her cheek. "Do you, Princess?"

When the baby was dressed and the queensguard let us know the Grand Dome was filled, Reece and I walked down the private corridor toward the huge gathering space.

He carried Sadie in one arm and with the other clasped my hand.

That was how we entered the Dome—together—a family.

And as I looked out over the assembly of other new families, of hopeful faces, of *people* I cared about, I knew the time had come.

It was time for *all* of us to leave the Bastion and join the world we had worked together to create through a combination of peace and power.

"My friends... thank you all for being here. It's so good to see each and every one of you. All of the life, all of the *love* in this room gives me so much joy I don't have the words to express it. Like many of you, Reece and I have extra reason to be joyful these days."

He stepped forward and lifted Sadie so everyone could see her.

"Meet Princess Sadie," Reece said.

There were cheers and applause mixed with oohs and aahs. Some of the other new parents held their babies up as well.

"I hope our daughter will have the chance to get to know and grow up with some of your children," I said. "As first generation, Crimson-born Americans, they share a connection like no other. But I don't want them to grow up *here*."

The room fell quiet.

"The Bastion is no longer necessary—and that's a *good* thing. The world is a better, safer place with enough room in it for vampires and humans alike. I encourage each of you to go out and explore it, claim a piece of it for yourselves, and take your rightful place in society."

People began looking around, as if in shock or in some cases, fear.

"There's no hurry," I assured them, "and no one will be forced to leave, but I want you to start considering the Bastion as more of a vacation destination, a site of historical interest, than a permanent home. It's time. The Crimson Accord is stronger than ever. You are *full* citizens with equal rights."

The faces looking back at me were so varied and each one so precious to me. Right now, not all of them were convinced.

I understood. Change was scary.

But I'd learned you didn't necessarily have to *stop* being afraid to move forward. The answer was to give yourself space to feel the fear… then simply to do what you needed to do even though you *were* still afraid.

That was how fear was defeated for good.

"Is the outside world perfect? No, but it's never been perfect," I said. "And President Parker will never be a great leader. But his threat against vampire-kind has been tamed. We'll be watching closely to make sure he doesn't backslide on his promises, and when his lame-duck single term ends, he'll fade into the sidenotes of history. As far as public opinion, not every mind will be changed. You know that. Some people will always hate those who are born different from them, who look different or have different cultural traditions. But hiding here is not the answer. It's only by working and living together and *listening* to each other that vampires and humans will come to truly know and understand each other."

I directed a significant glance at Shane and Marjorie, who'd fallen in love when she was a vampire and he was still human.

They stood, arm in arm, smiling back at me. She dropped a hand to her rounded belly, and he placed his atop it.

Beside them stood Kelly with her permanent mate, a Bloodbound soldier, and Heather with her hacker boyfriend, Luis.

He'd lasted longer than any of her paramours so far, so there was a chance even she *might* actually select a permanent mate of her own.

"I have immense hope for the future—for both our species," I told my people, and I meant every word. "I think more of us—humans and vampires alike—do believe love is preferable to hate, and *that* is enough for peace and goodwill to prevail."

Taking Reece's hand, I said, "Not all that long ago, when I was a scared little girl who'd never been outside her own village, someone said to me that there was no such thing as 'good enough,' that we should strive for *greatness* instead."

Reece beamed at me, tiny wrinkles forming at the corners of his eyes as he looked down at me with love.

I dragged my gaze away from him and our daughter to address the Bastion's citizens again.

"He also believed in destiny. *I* believe in my heart that he was right on both counts. Our destiny as a race, as a people, is to achieve greatness, each in our own way—and in ways we haven't even begun to anticipate yet. The possibilities are endless. The world is out there waiting for you. Make your mark on it. Change it for the better. Find *your* destiny."

THANK you for reading Crimson Crown! I hope you loved it and the entire Crimson series. If you enjoyed it, would you consider writing a quick review on your favorite book retailer's site?

There's no wrong or right way to write a review—a few words is all it takes, and reviews are very important. They help authors more than you know and help other readers find great books.

IF YOU MISSED a book in the series, turn to the Also By page for a list of all four books and the reading order.

Already read them all and hungry for more suspense, magic, and fantasy romance?

Be sure to check out my completed bestselling Hidden Saga series— perfect for a captivating, emotional, deeply romantic book binge. For a limited time, the ebook of the first in the series, **Hidden Deep,** is free!

Grab Hidden Deep now and give in to the glamor of the Hidden Saga. Keep reading for a sneak peek at the story…

AFTERWORD

Thank you so much for reading Crimson Crown, the fourth and final book in the Crimson Accord series. I hope you enjoyed it!

Never miss a new release when you join my VIP mailing list. List members receive early notification of my new books and audiobooks, sneak peeks, as well as fun freebies like The Sway, a novella set in the Hidden Saga world. I'd love to have you join and read it for free! Click here to do that.

If you haven't had the chance yet to Give in to the Glamor of the Hidden Saga, you can also read the first book in the series free! Hidden Deep is a full-length novel with fantastic reviews and hundreds of thousands of copies downloaded.

Here's a peek at the first chapter...

The first time I saw him, everyone convinced me he was a hallucination caused by hypothermia. It was the second time that messed me up.

It was only noon, but I couldn't wait anymore. The need to get out there had been growing stronger every day. With everything my mom had going on, maybe she wouldn't give me an argument this time. The screen door slammed behind me with a loud creak and double-bouncing bang.

"Ryann? You going out?"

I exhaled loudly then turned and faced my mother as she followed me out onto the back porch. She was dressed in her new red interview suit, a face full of going-somewhere makeup, and her hair up in clips where she'd been straightening it in sections. She'd rushed to the door in her stocking feet, causing a fresh run to start near her big toe.

"I left a note on the counter. Just going for a walk—you know." I shrugged. *No big deal.* Glancing down, I nodded toward her foot. "You'd better change those."

"Shoot!" She hiked up her skirt and started ripping off the pantyhose. "What the heck am I doing? I haven't worked in sixteen years. They're going to laugh me out the door."

She wobbled to one side, off balance. I reached out to steady her. "They'll love you."

Mom wrinkled her nose, brushing off my reassurance. "You're right. How could they not want such a strong job candidate? Thirty-six, living with my mother again, and did I mention the part about no work experience? Don't ever get yourself in this situation, Ryann. Depend on you—no one else—"

"Mom." I interrupted before she could launch into the full mantra. "They're going to love you."

She balled up the ruined stockings and gave me a doubtful smile, the shallow lines on her forehead deepening. Her eyes closed for a long moment, and she let out a resigned sigh. "Why do you want to go tromping around in those buggy, thorny woods every day, Ryann? You know I hate it."

"I won't go far. I'll probably be back before you even get home."

I knew exactly what this was about. In my mother's mind, I was still six years old, likely to wander off and get lost, and this time, never return. There was a pause, and I could see the surrender forming behind her eyes.

"Well… spray yourself so you don't get eaten alive." She picked up a can of insect repellant from the porch railing, thrusting it at me. "And stay on the trails. And don't be late."

"*You* don't be late." I took the can and smiled at her, already backing down the porch stairs. "And good luck."

Stepping out into the pine-scented heat was a relief. We'd moved way out into the sticks, but we hadn't left the tension behind in town. A giddy sense of freedom swept me up, and I practically ran to get to the trees bordering my grandma's house. My home now, too, as of three days earlier.

I'd come here for visits my whole life. Now it was a little more permanent, which was fine with me. I'd always loved this place. The hot clinging air, the rambling log house, and especially the deep, dense woodland surrounding it. The locals would probably think that was kind of strange, since most of them remembered when I nearly died out here.

Sticks snapped under my sneakers as I walked, listening to birdsong and whining insects. All familiar and welcoming. And a familiar feeling wrapped around me as well. Of hoping for… something. I wasn't sure what.

I'd promised not to go far, and I didn't intend to, but once I got going, it was too tempting to keep on walking, exploring deeper into the woods. The further I went, the lighter I felt. The sensation was like exhaling after holding your breath for way too long. Anyway, if I'd kept my promise and stayed on the trail, I never would've found this place.

The spring-fed pool was so clear I could see the large flat rocks and green plants lining the bottom. Leaves pirouetted from the surrounding trees, landing and floating on the glassy surface. Sunlight streamed through the treetops in little pockets, making a kaleidoscope pattern on the moss and springy wild ferns growing along the water's edge. It felt like my own magical discovery.

My t-shirt and shorts were plastered to me at this point, and my skin actually felt thirsty. Late May in Mississippi is not for wusses. Looking at the clear water, the idea of an outdoor bath started to seem too delicious to resist. It was kind of crazy—I mean, I hadn't exactly packed a swimsuit for my little nature walk. Whatever. I could use a minute or two of crazy in my life right about now.

I shucked my sweaty clothes, leaving my bra and panties on. There might have been six hundred acres of my grandma's posted forest land between me and the nearest person, but I wasn't *that* brave.

I stepped into the cool water. It felt unbelievably good, and I slipped under, blowing out all the stuffy humid air in my body. After a minute my lungs burned. I resurfaced, stood up in the waist-deep pool, and waited for the water to stop running down my face. Then I opened my eyes.

There in front of me, kneeling on the mossy bank and staring right at me, was a guy. A big blond guy, about my age.

I know him. No—wait—I don't know.

It didn't really matter because he shouldn't have been there. No one should've been there, but he was. *I'm basically naked and alone in the woods with a stranger. Not good.*

My chest was on fire. I wasn't breathing, and then I was breathing too much, too quickly. My mind spun and scrambled for anything like a rational thought. If I'd been watching myself in one of those stupid screamer movies, I'd have been shouting at the screen, "Move! Run! Do *something.*" But it was like that time when I was home alone and thought I heard an intruder. I just froze.

The guy looked almost as shocked as I felt, seeming unable to tear his wide-eyed stare away. Like me, he was frozen in place.

Then his face relaxed. And he smiled.

Sure. Alligators can smile, too. At least the sight ripped me out of my temporary paralysis. I finally moved, lunging toward the bank, intending to climb out and run, or at least get my clothes.

Oh. *My clothes.* I plunged myself back into the water up to my chin. I had no idea what to do. I was basically at this guy's mercy—miles from anyone who could hear me scream, ridiculously outsized and overpowered. He still hadn't said anything. No "I'm sorry," or "Hello there," or "Why no, I'm *not* a rapey stalker."

"Get out of here. You're trespassing." My attempt to be threatening came out sounding kind of pathetic, breathy and high-pitched.

The guy jerked back, lost his balance, and ended up on his rear. For a minute I was hopeful—maybe he was actually buying my bluff—but he got back up slowly to his haunches, and the corner of his mouth eased up along with one eyebrow.

"Trespassing? Well. There must be some law against public indecency, too. You shouldn't be out here like…" He gestured toward me. "…that."

His voice was deep, mature-sounding, though he wasn't more than eighteen, and his amused grin said he couldn't have been more pleased I *was* out here like this.

Who does he think he is? "No, you stupid ass—*you* shouldn't be out here. I own these woods, and You. Are. Trespassing. Now leave." That was it—I'd used the only cuss word I could pull off convincingly, and I sure did hope it worked, because if it didn't, I had nothin'.

My tough talk made me feel slightly less afraid. But I was

still stuck in the shamefully clear pool, and he was still there grinning and looking at me like the kid who'd found the Halloween candy stash.

He stood, and I had to squint up at him. His dark blond hair was haloed by the rays of sun slipping through the leafy canopy above. Strands of lighter gold glinted through the loose curls. I was cornered by possibly the world's most angelic-looking peeping Tom. Or serial killer. Neither thought was comforting.

Our standoff continued for long moments. Then suddenly he was moving toward me. He reached down and grabbed my pile of clothes on the bank and extended them out over the water to me. "Sorry," he said, not exactly sounding full of remorse, "but I'm not leaving. I need to talk to you first."

I willed myself to breathe again. "*Talk* to me? No. Just leave. Go away or…" Or what? I'd scream, and all the forest creatures would rush to my rescue? I'd stay in there until I shriveled like a Craisin?

He looked at me, waiting for me to finish my empty threat, I guess. When it was clear I wasn't going to, he narrowed his eyes and twisted his lips in a calculating expression.

"Okay. Listen, if you don't *want* these clothes, I'll toss them over there, and go sit down awhile against that tree. My arm's getting kind of tired." He stretched it to demonstrate his point, grinning widely at me again. If I could've reached him, and done it without giving him another free peep show, I'd have slapped that perfect smile off his face. So… maybe I wasn't dealing with someone dangerous here, but he sure was annoying.

I had a choice—argue with the guy holding the only thing standing between me and full-frontal, or stay there wearing my arms for a shirt and hope he'd eventually get bored and leave on his own. Right. I snatched the clothes out of his hand and scowled at him.

"Could you at least turn around?"

He paused a second then turned his back, and I set a world speed record for underwater dressing. Then I crept up the bank, grabbed my shoes, and took off running. He might have been harmless, but why take chances? I managed a few yards and didn't hear him coming after me. Then the huge golden-haired guy dropped out of a tree right in front of me.

I let out a squeal as my wet body slammed hard into his. He grabbed my upper arms, steadying me. I started screaming and slapping at him with my sneakers, dropping them in the process.

He immediately let me go and raised his hands in surrender. His words came out in a hurry. "Hey, calm down. I know I scared you. But I'm not going to hurt you. I only want to talk to you. Please."

I stepped back and rubbed my arms where his fingers had been moments earlier. "I guess you're not going to give me a choice. All right then. You want to talk? You go first. What are you doing on my land, and why were you spying on me?"

"Your land. Right. Well, I wasn't spying. I was walking back from the library." He nodded toward a scattered pile of books on the other side of the pool. "I saw your clothes and shoes there—I was going to keep going so I wouldn't scare you, but then you didn't come up for so long. I was just checking to see if you were okay. I didn't mean for you to see me. And then there you were, and you were all..." He swept his hand up and down in my direction and blushed deeply.

"Exposed? Half-naked? Don't try to make me believe *you* were embarrassed. Sorry, but I've got the market cornered on humiliation today."

"I'm sorry. Really. It's not like I planned this."

I studied him. Though I had no rational reason to believe

him, I did. Something in his voice told my self-preservation instinct to stand down.

"Okay then, assuming you're not a registered sex offender—you're not, are you?"

"No." He looked insulted.

"Unregistered?"

"No!" He gave a frustrated huff of a laugh.

"Okay. So you were walking back from the library... to where?" I thought of the few houses bordering my grandma's property. Most of the owners were old, like her. Maybe he was somebody's grandson, visiting for the weekend.

"I live... near here."

"Near here, like, off the county road, you mean?"

He glanced around. "Uh... yes."

Now that I was calm enough to care, I noticed he looked... different... not like any of the guys I'd ever seen in school. He was fresher somehow, healthier-looking, like no artificial color or flavor had ever crossed his lips. I couldn't decide if it was the skin or something else, but he looked like he'd never had a bad night's sleep. There were no freckles, no marks on him anywhere. His eyes were a pure, clear green, like sunlight shining through a leaf.

He wore ripped, faded jeans and an ancient plaid shirt with cut-off sleeves. It hung open to expose his smooth light brown chest and stomach. His feet were bare. It was like an Abercrombie ad gone wrong, because you didn't want to buy the clothes, just... him.

"You don't go to Deep River High. Did you just move here?" I had to ask—if I was going to have Spanish class next fall with a guy who'd seen me almost naked, I wanted to be forewarned. *Bonitas chichis, Senorita.*

"Oh, no, I uh... I'm home schooled."

"Good," I said quickly then slowed myself down. "I mean, all right. So what's your name?"

He hesitated but answered. "It's Lad."

"Okay then. Lad—I'm Ryann."

"I know."

Not what I was expecting to hear. I fired back at him, "How do you know my name?"

He looked away for a second then back at me. His eyes held a pleading I-know-I'm-busted look. He shook his head and opened his hands, palms-up to the sides. "I just... do?"

Wrong answer. I didn't care how cute he was, this was all too weird. I started backing away. "Well, um, Lad, now that we've *talked*, I have to get home. My mom and grandma are going to have the National Guard out here combing the woods soon."

He moved toward me and wrapped a large hand around my arm, the pressure not bruising, but firm. The heat of it sizzled on my wet skin.

"No. Not yet. Please, I have to show you something." He tilted his head down and stared directly into my eyes, lowering his voice. "You must come with me."

His gaze was so intense, almost like he was pushing me with his eyes, like he thought he could simply will me to agree with him. Right. My breath evaporated along with any feeling of comfort that had begun to develop. I leaned back, putting some space between us, and laughed nervously.

"You know what? The only thing I *must* do is get home. I'm not kidding about the National Guard. You've never met my mom or you wouldn't doubt it." I tried for flippant, but it came out sounding stressed.

"I can't let you go yet." He paused and then his tone turned up, like he'd just had a great idea. "I have something of yours. I want to give it back."

"What could *you* possibly have of *mine*? No thanks. I'm leaving." I wrenched my arm free, turned and stomped off, praying he didn't repeat that freaky dropping-from-the-branches move, and growing more nervous every second about this guy's inability to take no for an answer.

"I found your book."

His quiet words stopped me. I slowly turned to face him again, my stomach lined with ice. Finding the breath to respond was a challenge.

"What book?" But I already knew what he was going to say.

"The book you left out here… that night."

Ten years ago. "How do you know about that?"

"You can have it back. You want it, don't you?"

I did. More than that, I wanted to know how this stranger knew about my beloved childhood book. And what was he doing with it after all this time? There was really only one explanation.

"It's you, isn't it?"

He smiled and just looked at me, those scorching bright eyes like a magnifying glass over a dry leaf, burning a hole through everything I'd believed for the past ten years.

Grab your own copy of Hidden Deep now and keep reading!

THE COMPLETE CRIMSON ACCORD SERIES

Reading order:

Crimson Born

Crimson Storm

Crimson Bond

Crimson Crown

ABOUT THE AUTHOR

Amy Patrick writes "unique" and "engrossing" (Examiner. com) romantic fiction and young adult fantasy/paranormal books that make you want to "read straight through the night into the breaking hours of dawn." (Bitten By Books)

Her hugely popular Hidden Saga is now joined by her new Crimson Accord series, a young adult vampire romance saga.

Follow Amy on Bookbub to receive notices about her new releases and sales, and join her VIP mailing list at https://bit.ly/APsVIPs for the latest book news, insider info, and fun freebies.

Amy is a multi-award-winning author and two-time RWA Golden Heart finalist and lives in Rhode Island where she enjoys writing at the beach year round. She's been a professional singer, voiceover artist, and TV news anchor, and currently writes fiction full time as well as narrating audiobooks.

Keep in touch with Amy Patrick on Facebook, Instagram, Tiktok, Goodreads, Bookbub, and Pinterest!

For more, visit her website—
http://www.amypatrickbooks.com/

9 781946 166371